A SWITCH
IN TIME

A SWITCH
IN TIME

Judith R. Thompson

Authors Choice Press
San Jose New York Lincoln Shanghai

A Switch in Time

Authors Choice Press
an imprint of iUniverse.com, Inc.

For information address:
iUniverse.com, Inc.
5220 S 16th, Ste. 200
Lincoln, NE 68512
www.iuniverse.com

DISCLAIMER: This novel is a work of fiction. Any references to real people,
events, establishments, organizations or locales are intended only to give the
fiction a sense of reality and authenticity. Other names, characters, places
and incidents portrayed herein, are either the product of the author's
imagination or are used fictionally.

ISBN: 0-595-16822-1

Printed in the United States of America

To all who believe in angels, practice random acts of kindness, and trust in a higher source as I truly had help from above...

Acknowledgements

The Author wishes to thank my friend, Sharon Thompson (who is married to my ex) who helped me brainstorm and name my novel; to her husband, (and the dad to our daughter, Sonya) Gary, who kept their beautiful beach house in Avon, N.C., well stocked with food and brew, where the book was started; to our daughter, Sonya, for her inspiration, encouragement and loving support; to my parents, Barb and Dick Noonan, who just celebrated their 50th, for loving what they were reading; to my niece Alantra Letner, for her excitement, and my sister, Donna, my Aunt Emma for their similar interests. Their positive feedback kept it going. To Dan for his love and support and computer lessons. And I also want to thank my guardian angels, in particular, my writing muses, my great, great grandfather Arthur.

Introduction

It was a busy day in the Birthday Center in the hectic halls of Heaven. The Nanny angels were busy matching baby souls with potential parents down on Earth. It was a trying task as the Nanny angels had to match the waiting-to-be-born souls with a sex, time period, time zones, city, country, learning requirements, life schedules, life lessons, purposes, plans, needs, and wants to the waiting parents. Every soul had certain lessons that they needed to learn and master before they could go to the next life level.

There are many, many levels of life, both in physical form and in spiritual form. Only God can determine how many levels and which levels each soul needs to experience and complete before one is to truly join with Him.

The harried angels also had to go over each particular personal requisition sent to them directly from God and His council, and match all the orders as best they could. Things aren't as perfect up here as one would expect. After all, only God is perfect.

A newly appointed Nanny angel, Angela, was finding the task today particularly daunting. Angela very much wanted to prove herself worthy of this most important job. However, Angela was a bit dyslexic and tended to invert numbers. The Fore-Angel, Angelique, who was very experienced at her job, double-checked each angel's match. She realized early on that Angela might need more of her attention than some of the other Nanny angels. Angelique, more often than not, found the errors and corrected them before the match was in the final stage.

Today, however, was busier than normal. It was in the midst of the baby boomers generation. Generally this phenomenon occurs for several years after a war. More baby souls were needed to satisfy all the mating that had been going on down on Earth.

Angelique, the Fore-Angel, was so over loaded with match-ups that she missed checking two of Angela's assignments.

A baby soul, Hattie, was to be sent to a John and Mary Smith of Plymouth, Massachusetts, on May 11, 1891; and a baby soul Kaitlynn, was to be sent to a Bob and Jennifer Jones of Plymouth, New Hampshire, on May 11, 1981.

Well, the two baby girl souls were sent down the Birthing Tunnel on May 11th as scheduled.

In Heaven there is no time, as we know it on Earth. Everything happens simultaneously, on different levels in Heaven. The levels are designated by life lessons needed to be learned by each individual soul. For example: Some souls need to learn to live and love without, or with very little, material things. And some souls need to learn to live and love with an abundance of material things. This is just one of the millions of examples and levels.

By the time Angelique went over Angela's station to check on her schedule, the two female baby souls, Hattie and Kaitlynn, were already fighting their way through the vaginal tunnels of their perspective mothers.

1

Kaitlynn

May 11, 1891

It was a warm spring evening, on a small dirt lane, in a run down little farmhouse in the small town of Plymouth, Massachusetts. John Smith paced nervously outside the tiny gray clapboard home. Agonizing screams could be heard from inside the house. His wife, Mary, was in the process of giving birth to their first child. Her screams continually permeated the otherwise still night air. Each scream made John pace a little faster, sweat a little more. He was thankful that their neighbor, Sara, a mid wife, was here to help Mary with the birthing.

John was normally a quiet, stoic man who seldom showed much emotion. But as the screams and moans and groans of his wife continued getting louder and more frequent, his brow beaded and dripped with perspiration. He was a tall man, about six feet, still in his twenties. He had slightly thinning light brown hair. His blue eyes were bright with tears as he paced with worry and concern. He was fairly ignorant when it came to female problems. He was having a hard time trying to fathom how a baby arrives the way it does. Somehow, though, John knew that it had to be extremely difficult and painful.

Inside the small house, John's wife, Mary, was struggling with her last, she hoped, major labor push to expel the new life, fighting so hard inside her to get out. Mary was a petite, fair-haired woman. Her small size was definitely working against her. Being petite is great when it comes to clothes, shoes and snuggling beside her big tall husband, but it was a negative when having a baby. It hurt like hell!

The mid wife, Sara, a robust Irish woman, gently coaxed Mary. Sara knew how difficult having a baby is. She had had eight healthy children and had lived to brag about them all. Sara told Mary that the crown of the baby's head was showing.

Within minutes the baby was wailing.

"It's a girl!" exclaimed Sara to Mary.

"Thank God!" gasped Mary. "I wanted a daughter!"

John, hearing the baby cry, came running into their tiny sparsely furnished bedroom. Seeing both Mary and the new babe alive, he was all smiles.

"What are you going to call her?" asked Sara.

Mary, still panting from exhaustion, blurted out the name, "Kaitlynn!"

There was dead silence in the room. No one had ever heard of that name before. John was certain that the baby, if a girl, was to be named Hattie, after his deceased grandmother.

Even Mary was puzzled. It had also been her intention to name the baby Hattie. But being a very religious and superstitious person, she did not dare change the name. It was an old wife's tale, that once a baby's name has been heard by the baby's own ears, it must be. If the name was changed and the baby had already heard the first name spoken out loud, it would prove disastrous to the baby. The baby would be doomed to a life of confusion, constantly wondering about her identity and asking that annoying question, 'who am I?'

Lord knows the problems that could come from that.

Mary, therefore, trusted the old wives, whoever they were.

And so Kaitlynn Smith was born.

John and Mary Smith kept repeating the name…'Kaitlynn Kaitlynn', until it began to feel and sound all right.

2

Hattie

May 11, 1981

It was a cool spring night in a busy maternity ward at Lakes Regional Hospital in the small town of Plymouth, New Hampshire.

Bob Jones was trying to get his near hysterical wife, Jennifer, to calm down and breathe the way they had learned and practiced for months in the Lamaze classes they had taken. Bob was gowned and masked in the hospital paper gear and holding his wife's hand. Jennifer's Aunt Tanya, her mother's sister, was also gowned and ready to assist her favorite niece. Jennifer and Tanya were especially excited at the date of the up coming birth. May 11th was the same birthday as one of their most favorite, though now deceased, people in the whole world, 'Aunt Kate'. Jennifer had promised to name her first daughter after this dear family friend.

The Obstetrician and his nursing staff were all busy doing their various tasks in the labor room.

Jennifer, a thin anorexic woman, who barely looked pregnant, asked for some medication, as she could not tolerate the pain. Although she had read many baby books, seen the videos of birth, she was still unprepared for the physical pain. No book could adequately explain that.

The doctor gave her a spinal and her pain quickly subsided. Shortly after that, a baby girl was born. The umbilical cord was cut, the placenta pulled out and the baby was whisked away by a nurse to be checked and washed, and its nose and mouth cleared out. After all that was done, and the baby was wrapped in a soft, warm, pink blanket, she was placed in her mother's arms.

"What are you going to name her?" asked the smiling nurse, named Samantha.

Jennifer and Bob smiled and cried happy tears as they looked lovingly at each other. They had spent many hours thumbing through Baby name books, as they wanted a new unique Name for a son, but had already known what they would name a daughter.

"Hattie!" They both said at the same time.

Bob looked at Jennifer and Jennifer looked at Bob, puzzled and flabbergasted. Hattie did not sound like the name Kaitlynn that they had originally decided on. But, they were aware of the old wives' tale regarding the first name out, is a keeper, at least for the baby's sake. So just to be safe in case, they decided they better keep the name Hattie. After all, you do not take chances with an innocent baby. They weren't sure how much a little baby understands at birth. Some book said they know a lot at this age and others say they don't know much. But everything a mother did, even while pregnant, has an effect on the baby. At least that's what 'They' say. This is what Bob and Jennifer believed. They trusted the baby books.

So Hattie Jones was born.

3

Heaven

Meanwhile, up above, Angelique was giving Angela a very hard time about the now discovered mistake.

"Do you see how confused and surprised these parents are? What were you thinking?" Angelique asked Angela, with some exasperation.

"I'm so sorry. I have always had a problem with inverting numbers. I thought that once I got to Heaven all these kinds of problems would no longer exist," Angela answered feeling badly.

"Inverting numbers happens when you are in a hurry. Anyone can do that. You need to learn more patience. God must have thought that you were good enough to stay in Heaven, but you'll still need to work on your patience and pay more attention to details," Angelique explained.

"I do feel grateful that He allowed me to stay," said Angela meekly.

"You should feel grateful. We get many, many visitors who have just experienced a serious illness, accident or misfortune that arrive here before their time. Why, I remember two visitors not so long ago, a Betty Eadie and a Dannion Brinkley. Both of them had what Humans call 'a near death' experience, where they supposedly died and then were brought back to life by the impressive medical machines that have been developed on Earth. These machines, however, tend to interfere with some of God's plans. And when that happens and we receive an early visitor, God usually sends a relative, who died at the right time, to converse with them and explain to them, that they have to go back to Earth. That there is still more for them to do on Earth before God is ready to receive them here in Heaven. Sometimes God gives the untimely visitor a gift of knowing of future events, or a gift for healing, so that the visitor won't feel too badly about returning back to Earth. Both Eadie and Brinkley returned to Earth and wrote very important books describing their visits here. These books EMBRACED BY THE LIGHT and SAVED BY THE LIGHT, were in God's plan, as there are many problems on Earth that need spiritual growth and knowledge to help the Humans to overcome some of these very negative and detrimental problems that are happening on Earth as we speak."

"There are no free rides! Even up here. We always strive to become more God-like. Our work is never done, " explained Angelique.

Angela nodded her head in agreement. She felt extremely thankful, and praised God for allowing her to continue her growth in Heaven instead of Earth. She then asked her Fore-Angel, Angelique, "What do you think will happen to Kaitlynn and Hattie?"

"God only knows," said Angelique, shaking her head with some concern. "This is one of those weird coincidences; two girls, same birthday, same town name…" Angelique went on.

"Well, I remember a book called CELESTINE PROPHESY, that I read while I was on Earth. It said that there were no coincidences," Angela said.

"You can't believe everything you read. One thing I do know, there is a reason for everything. And I am sure God has His Plan with this mix up. We'll just have to watch carefully and see what happens, "murmured Angelique. "We're all born with some foreknowledge so that we can better adapt to the time we spend on Earth. This foreknowledge could present some problems for Kaitlynn and Hattie. We'll just have to wait and see.

4

Kaitlynn

1893

Kaitlynn Smith was well in to her second year of life on Earth. She had begun to walk just before her first birthday. She also learned to talk at about that same time. Her parents were amazed at her progress, as most of their friends' children were much slower to walk and talk.

Kaitlynn had developed an annoying habit of throwing her soiled cloth diaper away. Her mother, Mary, would retrieve the diaper from the trash pile located behind the barn, and wash and scrub it by hand and hang it out to dry.

Kaitlynn could not understand why her mother wasted so much time doing this dirty chore. She thought it would be a lot easier if her diapers were disposable. Just the thought of re-wearing a previous messy diaper irked Kaitlynn. But then she did not like using a chamber pot or accompanying her mom to the smelly cold out house either. She thought it would be nice if she could have a small chair-like potty to sit her little pink bum on. But she was only two. What did she know and what could she do about it?

Kaitlynn was already talking quite well for a toddler. The 'whys?' Had started early, much to her parents' dismay.

John would constantly ask his wife to explain to him what this little girl was talking about. Kaitlynn constantly asked if she could go to McDonald's. John knew that there were no neighbors near them by that name.

Kaitlynn did not like much of the food her parents made her eat; mush, oatmeal, gruel and stews. She felt her mom spent too much at the old wood stove. The oven was hot, dirty and burnt a good deal of their meals.

Kaitlynn would have preferred a boxed cereal with pretty colors and a sweet taste for breakfast.

In spite of the food problems, Kaitlynn was a happy, curious and precocious child. She had pretty curly blonde hair, sparkling, mischievous teal-blue eyes and a tiny rosy mouth.

She seemed to have developed considerably faster than many of her cousins. Secretly Mary was very pleased and delighted with this perky, though puzzling little girl.

When Kaitlynn would ask for a soda, her mom would happily give her a soda cracker and then wonder why her darling daughter would look so quizzically at it. Kaitlynn would then ask her mom for a juice-in-the-box. Mary would drop what she was doing and go get one of Kaitlynn's few toys, a jack-in-the-box. Mary would give it to Kaitlynn who would then put the toy up to her pursed little lips. Then patiently, Mary would get down on the rough hand hewn floorboards and show Kaitlynn how to wind the box up. Mary thought it was cute the way Kaitlynn always kissed it first. Kaitlynn, on the other hand, would get frustrated because she was thirsty. Finally her mom would figure it out and get a drink of milk or water.

Although much in little Kaitlynn's world was confusing to her, she still seemed to be enjoying herself and growing well.

5

Hattie

1983

Hattie Jones, now a little over two years old, had wavy red hair and big green eyes, which seemed to always be wide, open. She had a constant perplexing look of awe on her small ruddy face. She was particularly interested and amazed by light bulbs, pictures on the television, the beeping sounds from the computer on her mom's desk and anything animated, bright or shiny. Every time the phone would ring, Hattie would jump, feel startled and then clap her hands with excitement.

Her parents were a bit concerned that Hattie was showing signs of becoming a couch potato. She was so enamored by the television. She didn't sing or dance or interact with Sesame Street, or any of the other children's shows. She just sat there staring and staring. What Hattie was really doing was wondering when the little people in the TV box would come out to play with her. She stared with equal intent at commercials, newscasts, talk shows, sporting events, MTV, etc., etc.

Hattie had begun to talk, but with great difficulty. It was almost like she didn't understand what she was saying.

The only time she seemed to be a fairly normal child was when LIT-TLE HOUSE ON THE PRAIRIE came on television. Every time she saw Michael Landon and the lady that played his wife, Hattie would say, "Mommy, daddy on TV."

Bob and Jennifer got a kick out of that, but explained that mommy and daddy were here in the den with Hattie, not on television.

Hattie had some other odd quirks. She preferred to go outside when she needed to pee or poop. It was almost like she was afraid to smell up the house and was frightened of the toilet.

Jennifer thought that it was cute, but would try to explain to Hattie that she could go to the bathroom any time she wanted to because she had disposable diapers.

Hattie was very slow to potty train.

Hattie also preferred to still eat her hot oatmeal cereal over a family trip to a hamburger joint or pizza parlor. She liked quiet meals in a dim lit room. McDonald's and the Pizza Hut were too noisy and busy. There was too much to see and wonder about. Hattie could not eat in such distracting environments.

Jennifer figured that her daughter was just shy and overly sensitive and did not like to eat in front of strangers. Her father joked about it, telling his wife that they will be able to save a lot of money by eating in, instead of eating out all the time, like all their yuppie friends.

Hattie tended to make things more difficult for herself. She always cried when her mom or dad changed her diaper and threw it away. She cried when her parents threw anything away.

Hattie had already begun to take on the characteristics of a pack rat. She wanted to save everything, just in case. She was very frugal.

Her parents also kept their television on most of the time because Hattie would cry and yell very loud when the TV was turned off. In her little baby mind she thought it hurt all the people inside the box.

6

Heaven

Angela was getting better at her job in the Birthday Center in Heaven. She hadn't made any serious mistakes like she had a while ago with those two little baby girl souls.

She did, however, from time to time, pop down to Earth to see how Kaitlynn and Hattie were doing. Except for some minor adjustment problems, both Kaitlynn and Hattie seemed to be in good families and had good health. The parents seemed to have adjusted very well with their switched daughters. (What they didn't know could not hurt them.)

Knowing this made Angela happy. Even God had forgiven her this 'wee' mistake.

After all, there were a lot of baby souls who went to much worse situations. Some of her poor babies, (she tended to think all her assignments as her babies.), went to terribly dysfunctional families and horrible time eras. Many suffered atrocious tragedies. Why these little children had to learn some of these horrible lessons, like the millions of little babies that had to be sent to the gas chambers in Germany and Austria, and the millions of black babies that had to learn of discrimination and famine, the millions that have painful incurable diseases or had horrendous handicaps of blindness and deafness or are crippled in any way, or the millions that had to suffer gender problems, or had to suffer child abuse, or incest and rape or had to starve to death, etc., etc. was far beyond her knowledge and understanding.

Well, it wasn't Angela's job to wonder why. She had great faith and love in God's plan. And she did know that eventually all God's children would eventually be reunited with Him.

With that thought in mind, Angela didn't worry too much about Kaitlynn and Hattie. They had it better than most. Besides, she'd be keeping a watchful eye over them, just in case. She was pulling double duty as their special Guardian Angel. (We should all be so lucky.)

7

Kaitlynn

1901

Kaitlynn was now ten years old. She was maturing very quickly. Her vocabulary and knowledge far surpasses her fellow classmates. She attended a one-room schoolhouse with thirty other students of all different ages. There were several students older than her, but she was smarter than all of them.

Her thirst for knowledge was insatiable. She read every book she could get her hands on. Her curiosity was unwaning. Her appetite was voracious. Whenever she finished reading a book, she would sense a feeling of dejavu, like she had already been there, done that.

Regardless of what seemed to be her inner knowledge, she still loved to read. Kaitlynn had already read most of Shakespeare, Dickens, Louisa May Alcott, Thoreau, Emerson, E.E. Cummings and Poe, as well as every other book she came upon.

Kaitlynn was so thirsty for knowledge that her teachers had a hard time keeping up with her and would jokingly tell Kaitlynn that she should be teaching them.

Because of Kaitlynn's seemingly studious nature, she had a hard time making friends. Kaitlynn found most kids her age somewhat boring. All the girls seemed to want to do was play with dolls or play cowboys and Indians with the boys. Kaitlynn could not relate to such frivolity.

At home with her mom and dad, she was a great help. When her parents would ask her to do a chore like scrub the floor, white wash the fence, make soap, can vegetables, feed the farm animals etc., etc., she would take on each chore at full throttle. Kaitlynn was almost (dare I say) a workaholic. Except for when she was sleeping or reading, she was constantly moving and doing. She was a real mover and a shaker.

Many times her mother, Mary, would tell her to slow down and spout adages like 'haste makes waste,' or 'stop and smell the coffee.' But not Kaitlynn. Her main thought was that there were too few hours in every day. She never had enough time to do everything she wanted to do. She had an uncanny sixth sense that constantly told her she had to catch up. Catch up to what, she had no idea.

Another very odd thing about Kaitlynn was that even when she was busy, busy, busy, she would occasionally stop in her tracks and stare up into the sky, wishing that she could fly. Sometimes she would entertain her mom and dad at the supper table with her dreams of flying some day.

"Don't you wish you could fly like a bird?" Kaitlynn would ask dreamily.

"Don't be silly," her mom would reply. "If God had meant for us to fly, He would have given us wings."

Her dad, John, would just chuckle and shake his head as he ate his hard earned supper.

"Well, some day I might be able to fly. I might be able to fly to England across the Atlantic Ocean and visit some of our old relatives you're always talking about," Kaitlynn would prattle on. "Why, I bet some day, I could even fly to the moon."

"Hush child. Finish your supper. Stop this nonsense," her father would finally say.

Kaitlynn did as she was told, as she was a good daughter, although her parents considered her somewhat flighty. (Pardon the pun.) But Kaitlynn still dreamed of flying someday.

Another problem Kaitlynn had was that she wanted to wear pants like her father instead of the homespun cotton dresses and pinafores her mom made her wear every day. She felt that pants would be more appropriate when she was helping with all the farm chores. She argued almost daily with her mom about the practicality of wearing pants instead of dresses.

Her mother eventually tired of this on going debate with her daughter and gave in to Kaitlynn. Mary made several pairs of pants for Kaitlynn, with the strict instruction that she was not to go into town with pants on. She was not to embarrass her parents in public. Kaitlynn reluctantly agreed.

8

Hattie

1991

Hattie was ten and having trouble at school. She had had to repeat the fourth grade and could not continue on to the middle school with all the friends she had known since Kindergarten.

She was held back because she could not grasp modern math, science or the use of computers and calculators. All of it just baffled her.

She also seemed to be constantly stressed and agitated. Every time there was a catastrophe broadcast on television, such as when the Challenger space shuttle exploded in 1986, Hattie became so distraught and miserable for months afterward. Her parents tried to curb her fascination with the televised newscasts, but to no avail. Being a modern family, there were televisions in almost every room of the house. And even as upset as Hattie would get whenever something terrible was aired, she would feel worse if she couldn't find out the end result of a story, good or bad.

Hattie was having a very difficult time adjusting. Being so sensitive (and technically, out of her element, so to speak), most of the modern equipment, information and classes at school were too much for her to take in and process at the same rate as most of her peers. She was considered 'slow' by her teachers.

When she was younger, her mom, Jennifer, would take Hattie antiquing. Jennifer and Bob, as modern as they were, had a great fondness for antiques. In one of the old musty barn antique shops, Hattie had come upon a weird looking thing called an abacus. Hattie didn't know why, but she had to have it. Hattie was so insistent about wanting it that Jennifer bought it for her, wondering all the while what the heck did her daughter want it for.

Hattie explained to her mom that it was an old fashion calculator. She proceeded to show her mother how it worked. Her mom was amazed that Hattie knew what to do with the abacus. Hattie could do her arithmetic with it so much easier than with a digital calculator and nearly as fast. Unfortunately, because Hattie's teacher didn't know how to use the abacus, Hattie wasn't allowed to bring it to school with her. But because of the abacus, Hattie started doing better in math and secretly, her teacher was quite impressed. But since it did not conform to the school's requirements, Hattie was still held back.

Another time, while antiquing, Hattie made her mom buy her an old kerosene lantern. Hattie loved this lamp and put it on her bureau in her bedroom. She even got her father to make it work and now she used it nightly. Hattie preferred the dim light to the brightness of electric lamps.

Hattie loved antiquing with her mother. For some strange reason she always felt peaceful and at home when she was around that old stuff in those old dusty barns.

Her mom would tease her and tell her that she was ten going on one hundred. Well, sometimes Hattie understood exactly what her mom meant. She often did feel old compared to her friends. It was a funny yet comfortable feeling.

Her girlfriends loved playing with their Barbie dolls and the cars and dollhouses and all the clothes that went with the Barbie dolls. Hattie also had several Barbie and Ken and Skipper dolls, but she preferred to make the doll clothes for them instead of buying the outfits in the department stores. She had learned to sew at an early age. Her grandmother taught her. She had even learned how to do petit point, crochet and knit. Hattie loved using her hands that way and spent hours sitting in an old rocker that her mom had bought because Hattie had to have it. She sat and rocked and sewed by the light of her kerosene lamp. Often she would make, what her friends called 'granny dresses and bonnets' for her Barbie and Skipper dolls.

Hattie wished that she could have a pretty blue gingham granny dress with a white pinafore. But her mom did not sew and would only shop at Sears, JCPenney and Walmart, and buy OshKosh, Levi's and other brand name clothes.

Hattie was smart enough to realize that she kind of had to dress like the other kids because she knew they would pick on her if she didn't. She didn't like how mean some kids could be to anyone who didn't look or act or dress the way they all did. So in that way she tried to fit in.

Hattie had a kind, sweet nature. She rather liked people who were different. After all, she sure felt different. Heck, she knew she was different. She also felt more at ease when she was around her grandmother and her friends. She enjoyed listening to the older people talk about the good old days. Although her grandmother and mother refused to talk about Hattie's grandfather. The subject was taboo.

Many times during dinner when her mom and dad were rushing around after having just gotten home from working all day, Hattie would tell her parents how she wished she could be a pioneer woman. She would go on and on about how she wished they could all live on a little farm out in the country.

Her dad, Bob, would tell her 'to get with the program'. He would also tell her how hard life was back then and how much easier life was now.

But as Hattie sat at the glass chrome dining table in big overstuffed modern contemporary chairs, eating her Stouffer's frozen dinner that was heated in the microwave, listening to her dad go on and on about how difficult life was back then, Hattie could only silently disagree and daydream about how wonderful the past all sounded to her.

9

Heaven

Angela was becoming concerned about her two girls, as she now referred to Kaitlynn and Hattie. They were beginning to show some signs of adjustment problems.

She pondered about what she maybe could do to help them adapt better to the times that she had mistakenly goofed up on. She knew that there must be something she could do to make their lives easier, but she couldn't quite put her finger on any particular solution.

Angela decided that she might have to go to a higher source to help her with this dilemma. She went to her Fore-Angel, Angelique, to ask for some guidance.

Angelique told her that she would have to make an appointment with one of God's right hand council members.

These council members were renown for their wisdom, righteousness and profound capabilities of solving difficult life problems. After all, many members on God's council had left quite an impression on Earth.

It seemed when Earth was having a crisis of major magnitude, one of these council members would volunteer to go back to Earth as a baby and live another life to help solve the many many problems. Some of the council members have lived multiple lives under the names of Plato, Ghandi, Martin Luther King, and John F. Kennedy, John Lennon, George Burns, George Washington, Abraham Lincoln, Joan of Arc,

Albert Einstein, Marie Curie, Louis Pasteur, Ben Franklin, Tom Jefferson, Tom Edison, Florence Nightingale, Socrates, Eli Whitney, Susan B.Anthony, Moses, Jesus, Booker T. Washington, Helen Keller, Anne Frank, Aristotle, Leonardo Davinci, Bach, Beethoven, Mozart, Picasso, Shakespeare, Alexander Graham Bell, Henry Ford, Clara Barton, Darwin, Harriet Beecher Stowe, Princess Diana, and Mother Teresa-and thousands of other brave souls who made great contributions to the Human Condition on Earth.

God considered his volunteers, any spirit who chose to go to Earth, of great importance. These courageous souls keep God's Plan on its course. They are regarded with great honor and respect.

Even the bad Humans like Hitler, Stalin, Ayatollah Khomeini, Judas, Jeffrey Dahmer, Ted Bundy, Jim Jones, L.Ron Hubbard, David Cresch, etc., etc. Have their place in God's grand scheme. (However, I am not the messenger in that regard. I don't know the Plan.)

Angela made her appointment. Now all she had to do was wait.

10

Kaitlynn

1906

Kaitlynn is now fifteen and has finished her schooling. She desperately wanted to go to college. Her parents, however, had different plans for her.

For one thing, her dad, John, told her that women didn't need a higher education, and in the early 1900's very few women went on to college. If they did go on, it was usually to a finishing school where they could learn to sew, play music, paint and work on their manners. Usually only the wealthy could afford such a luxury.

Money was one concern, but the other was that college was considered a man's domain.

Kaitlynn's mom was starting to tell her about the role of a wife and mother. Kaitlynn already knew all this and didn't like hearing about it. She heard about the woman's role all the time in church. She was sick of hearing how the women must obey the man and stand quietly behind him; that the man made all the decisions and rules and the woman had to adhere to them.

There were just too many things that Kaitlynn wanted to do and picturing herself settling down in a marriage and having lots of children were not on her list.

Several of Kaitlynn's friends were already married, getting married or planning on it in the near future. She would go with her friends to the church suppers and barn dances, and under the watchful eyes of their parents, would flirt and dance with the local boys. But none of the local boys were appealing to Kaitlynn. She thought them immature and moronic.

All the boys wanted was to get married, have lots of children and either work on there Daddies' farms work in town and, well, basically live the life their fathers lived.

Kaitlynn, at least, wanted to go west and see some of the rest of the world. With all the reading she had done over the years, it left her curious and wanting more than just the life that she saw around her.

She tried to explain her aspirations and dreams to her mother. Her Mother would listen for a little while, but then would take Kaitlynn down a peg or two by telling her about the real world of 1906 in Plymouth, Massachusetts. Mary would also tell Kaitlynn how important motherhood and being a good wife was.

Kaitlynn let the conversation go in one ear and out the other. She wasn't buying any of it. She thought her parents were being grossly unfair to her. She was not going to settle for her mother's way of life. She wanted more. She needed more. And 'by George' she was going to make sure that she got more.

11

Hattie

1996

Hattie was having a hard time in high school. Many of her classmates had pink, red, green or blue hair. Many had pierced their noses, eyebrows, lips, tongues and even their belly buttons. Tattoos were also the rage. Hattie could not understand the weirdness of all these fads. It made her think of Indians donning their war paint while preparing for battle. She supposed, though, with all the gang wars and killing of kids going on now a days, perhaps her classmates were getting ready for battle.

Some of the girls she knew were already having sex with their boyfriends. They even bragged about it. This shocked her. Hattie was terrified at just the thought of sex. There were so many talk shows on television that constantly alerted every one about the dangers of promiscuous sex, such as AIDS, STDS, and unwanted pregnancies.

Hattie was very naive about all of this, as she tended to tune the negative stuff out. It scared and intimidated her. She knew that she wanted to be pure and chaste and a virgin for her future husband.

She went to church regularly, much to her parents' surprise, as they did not believe in man-made organized religions. Hattie had heard several bad stories about organized religions and the danger that some of them represent. Hattie's mom had had a horrible run in with a cult religion called Scientology. It had happened while Jennifer was at her first real job in a computer software company. The Church of Scientology often and covertly ran businesses and other seemingly ordinary-type organizations, as a way to recruit new members into the cult. It was done by a very subtle, unassuming form of brain washing. (One would have to experience being brain washed to truly understand the sneakiness of it all.) It was done with information, technology over load. They would pay above average wages to hook young, up and coming employees with promises of a great future. They would insist that one worked far and beyond the call of duty, becoming highly trained, stressed-out workaholics. And then, very unsuspectingly 'train' their employees by a process called 'hatting.' Their subversive methods of handling insubordinates or anyone that tried to get out of some of these training sessions, were extremely degrading and demoralizing, either by demotions or odd punishments like reading many chapters of direct text from their leader, L.Ron Hubbard, which were hidden by calling his text Administrative Technology. In fact the only difference in this so-called religion is the omission of the word scientology and the replacement word, administration.

It was a horrendous experience for Jennifer, and an ordeal that left Hattie's mom very leery about all organized religions. Jennifer believed that all religions were man-made, and having seen first hand how treacherous 'men' could treat other human beings, she steered clear of all religions. Jennifer tried to instill in Hattie this caution. Jennifer had also learned how easy an unsuspecting, trusting young mind could be controlled by a very sinister group of people. Jennifer believed that freedom of one's mind was the only true freedom that one had. After her close call with scientology, she vowed to stay clear from anyone, or anything that attempted to control her.

But she also knew that Hattie had to learn some things on her own. Jennifer would keep a watchful eye on her only daughter. So she relented, somewhat, and let Hattie go to the church of her choosing, which in this case was the Catholic Church. At least she wasn't smoking, drinking or doing drugs. Hattie didn't hang around or belong to any gangs. She was a good kid.

Her parents knew that their daughter was very different compared to their friends' and neighbors' kids. She was such a good and healthy kid, that they didn't worry too much about the way she didn't quite fit in. She just walked to a different beat of the drum. In fact, they tended to like her originality. It was actually rather refreshing, not to mention, a relief, to not have to fret about her the way their friends worried about their kids.

The main two things that they did worry about were that Hattie did not want to go to college. All she wanted to do some day was get married and have three or four children. Bob and Jennifer wanted her to go to college. Everyone needed a college education these days. But they figured that maybe, if Hattie married a doctor or a lawyer or someone financially well off, she'd have a good life.

The other thing they worried about was Hattie's unrelenting interest and obsession with the OJ Simpson murder trial. Even though the trial had been over since November 1995, and OJ was acquitted of murdering his estranged wife, Nicole, and her friend, Ron Goldman, Hattie still watched every commentary show like Rivera Live and CNN's Larry King that continued to discuss the trial and the ramifications of the unpopular jury decision. Hattie also read every book that came out as a result of the trial.

Hattie's parents did not understand her fascination, especially now that the trial was over. Hattie, who, as a rule, seemed to dislike and react so emotionally over tragic events, was still drawn to watching them on television. This contradiction of her otherwise old fashion self, confused and mystified her parents.

Hattie couldn't explain her interest in the case either. She just knew that things weren't working right in the world today. She did believe that OJ was guilty and should have gone to prison for the rest of his life. She felt that the justice system was screwy. And she was upset at all the racial tension fall-out. It just didn't make sense. She was trying to make sense out of it, but it was difficult. But then, to Hattie, a lot of things these days didn't make any sense.

She had also been extremely upset over the senseless bombing of the Oklahoma City Federal Building, and Waco, and all the unnecessary deaths related to these events. Why would anyone do such a thing? And especially in America?

These current events really affected Hattie's peaceful sensitive nature. They incensed her inner moral code and ethical soul.

Her fascination with these atrocities was just as much out of awe as it was interest in wondering why people do the things they do. Why is the world so messed up? She did not feel comfortable in the modern world. That was one reason why she went to church. She needed to feel some peace. She longed for easier simpler times. She was going to do her damnedest to find a simpler life for herself, even if she had to resort to the old hippie-commune way of life of the 60's and 70's. She liked the idea of organic farming and using herbs, massage, acupuncture, and meditation to heal oneself. She liked the thought of natural childbirth and breast-feeding her children. In an odd way Hattie was very 'New Age.'

She was determined to give her children that she hoped for in the future, a better life. They would be raised in a kinder, gentler, quiet manner, much different than the hectic fast pace she was raised in.

If her parents did make her go to college she decided that she would either be a teacher or a nurse. She had no desires to make lots of money or to live in the fast lane, or anywhere nears the fast lane.

12

Heaven

Angela's appointment with one of God's council members went fairly well. She had explained her error of mixing up two female souls a while back and the difficulties both girls were experiencing in their reversal roles.

The council member that Angela had met with was a wise old soul. This spirit had spent its time on Earth thousands of years ago when the human civilization was just beginning to get on track. This spirit had probably reincarnated dozens of times in order to have learned all the lessons God needed it to learn. In other words, this wise old spirit had earned its wings. This spirit had had many lives as both male and female. So it was well versed and well educated in both sexes and their particular issues.

The wise and trusted spirit told Angela that there was much good to be found in both the new and old ways of mankind. It showed very little concern in the two girls' dilemmas.

"They will find their way, because that is God's way," the spirit told Angela. "All you need to do is give them a gentle nudge now and then if they stray too far off their life's path. Let them learn the lessons that have been predestined for them. Your job is not to interfere. If the girls should pray or voice their own personal concerns or wants or desires, God will hear. He will let you know when and if you need to step in. In the mean time, I am sure that you have a few issues of your own that still need work. Have the faith that God knows all things, and that all His children will eventually join Him," said the spirit in it's soothing and knowing telepathic voice.

Angela was calmed by the wisdom she heard, and thanked the spirit for its time and attention. She then went on with her heavenly life and duties.

13

Kaitlynn

1911

Kaitlynn was now twenty and considered an adult woman.

Her parents, John and Mary, were becoming extremely agitated and concerned that Kaitlynn still had not met her future husband and settled down. They constantly introduced her to sons of friends in their community. Kaitlynn would abide by her parents wishes and meet these men. She even went on an occasional date, but she found none of them interesting enough. She was not about to settle down, at least not yet.

Secretly Kaitlynn had been making her own plans for her future. She had managed to save enough money for a train trip across America. She wanted to check out California. She had read all about the gold rush, the San Francisco earthquake and fires of 1906, and all the new cities that were being developed all across the United States. She had read that the sun shone almost every day in California and the weather there was considered near perfect year round.

After many brutally cold and snowy winters and the coinciding hardships that came with these rough winters that she had experienced her whole life in Plymouth, Massachusetts, she was ready and craved a change in temperature. She wanted a different pace of life.

If she couldn't have a college education, she could damn well choose self-education and a different climate. Kaitlynn also decided that once she got to California she would get herself a dog. She was smart enough to know that even as independent as she felt she was, she would need some form of protection. She figured that a dog would serve the purpose better than any old guy could.

Kaitlynn wished that she could fly to California. She just knew that some day it would be possible to fly coast to coast. Especially since she had heard about Orville and Wilbur Wright's first successful controlled, man powered, 120' flight a few years ago in 1903 in Kitty Hawk, North Carolina.

At any rate, her plans were made. She just had to figure out how and when to break the news to her unsuspecting parents. She knew that they would be terribly upset and disappointed and probably scared shitless about her plans. After all, they expected that she would settle down and live practically next door to them. But Kaitlynn knew she had to do what she had to do. There was an inner voice telling her to 'go West, young woman, go West!'

14

Hattie

2001

Hattie was in the throes of a deep depression. The world was just moving too fast for her. She could not keep up with all the changes, both technically and personally, that seemed to be happening on a daily basis. She was only twenty years old, but she felt her youth was being zapped from her.

The world economy had become almost totally automated. There was no such thing, any more as paper money, or so it seemed. Most transactions were done with plastic cards or by computers. Only the people who use to save pennies and all their change were now collecting the last of the paper money. It was occasionally still found in some of the older, smaller towns or countries.

A person no longer even gets to see their paycheck. Computers automatically transfer everything. A pay voucher was given for personal record keeping. Once the paycheck had been deposited in a bank, or a money control center, all one had to do if one wanted to buy something or pay a bill, was to punch a code number and the receiver's code number and the amount of money was transferred. This was done on a wristwatch phone-computer, ATM combo unit that everyone had to have.

Hattie hated doing business this way. She had an inbred distrust of computers and the people who did nothing but operate them, especially the ones in the banks. These people seemed like machines or robots and even acted like that. They spoke very monotone with no emotion or feeling what so ever.

There had also been many international scandals involving huge amounts of money being embezzled by several mysterious computer hacks that had managed to figure out many of the big banks codes by bypassing specific satellite beams.

Hattie saw all this new fangled stuff as very detrimental to the human spirit. Even though many newly invented or improved items made life easier, like the new picture view wrist Cellular phones that were now being issued at birth with one's social security number and personal phone number that would stay with each person their whole life. A person could call anyone, anytime anywhere with great ease. However, the huge multi-plex data centers needed now to handle this 'piece of jewelry' seemed to have almost total control over everyone's life.

Hattie did not like this. She was too self sufficient and hated turning over personal information such as her medical history, employment history, credit history, and well, just your whole damn personal history. It felt intrusive. It was intrusive. And it was mandatory.

One of the few good things about it all is that people were becoming a bit more careful of not doing any thing illegal or unethical. Well, some people any ways. No one wanted the central control people to know if one ever took drugs, smoked, drank, had multiple sex partners, had cancer or any pre-disposed health or genetic problems; or shop lifted, lied or cheated in school or at work. People tended to be a lot more conscientious of the right or wrong of many decisions and choices they now made. Hattie supposed that that was a good thing.

It was amazing what a complete stranger could find out about you and/or knew about you. It was down right scary.

Hattie, although now twenty, was barely out of high school as she had been held back a couple of times, mostly due to her difficulty of grasping math and science courses. And because math and science was considered so necessary now a days, Hattie had to learn it.

She felt like she was totally spinning around, lost in space. She did not fit in. She was not ready and did not want her whole being to be run and controlled by computers or machines. It did not feel right or normal to her. She liked doing things from scratch, making her own clothes, cooking with natural ingredients, instead of everything being pre-packaged or frozen.

She was sure that all of this new technology just added to her depression. And now the fact that she's been labeled mal-adaptive, depressed (and god knows what else) and has been on anti-depressant medication and had to go to therapy twice a week, she was sure that all of her personal information was now out there, like dirty laundry, for all the world to see. She felt that it would destroy any future plans she had of finding a husband. Who would want her now?

In order to get married now a days a fiancée had every right to see your compute files, or data diary, and especially the files regarding your virginal status and/or how many sexual partners, male or female, a person may have had. The files also show if you ever had a sexually transmitted disease or was HIV Positive or, God forbid, had full blown AIDS. People were 100% more selective and more careful to marry. But Hattie thought that this was a good thing. Better safe than sorry.

There still was no cure yet for AIDS. With all the major medical advances that have been made so far in the 21st century, AIDS just seemed to go on and on, and got more and more complex. It continued to spread through out the world.

Hattie figured there must be a reason for AIDS. Like maybe the population growth needs to be slowed down because the planet Earth cannot handle too many more people. So maybe it was God's way of slowing every one's sexual urges down. Hattie had grown very spiritual, as she had studied many of the old religions.

As depressed as Hattie was, marriage was the last thing she worried about. She really didn't care about much right now.

Her parents, Bob and Jennifer, were terribly concerned, but they were still too busy working for a living and dealing with the stresses of their own lives. They did very little to help Hattie with her problems, or her future. They knew she didn't want to go to college so they had stopped pushing her in that direction. They figured that something would come up.

Secretly, Hattie's mom liked having Hattie at home. Hattie took care of the laundry, dishes and house cleaning. Having a daughter who would do all this was a rarity these days.

Hattie didn't particularly mind living at home and not working. She did think of herself as a spinster. A few years ago she couldn't wait to get married, but all the boys she thought were cute and liked, were more interested in pursuing their college degrees and securing a career for themselves. Very few of the guys, if any, seemed interested in marrying or having children. They didn't seem to care whether or not they had a son to carry on their name. A family just didn't seem as important in society today like it use to be in the good old days.

Hattie had hard time thinking about, let alone planning, her future. She felt she was already living in the future and she did not like it.

A few years ago Hattie had gotten hooked on calling the Psychic Phone-lines. She had been fascinated with the concept of some one being able to foresee hers or any one else's future. Some of the psychics were really good or so she thought at the time. Some of the psychics found Hattie confusing because what they thought was Hattie's future looked like Hattie's past. None of the psychics she had contacted could figure that out, so they just gave her some run of the mill predictions; 'you'll marry the man of your dreams, have two kids and make lots of money.' None of which has come true yet. But Hattie had faith in the psychics. She believed that what they told her would come true...some day. She could wait.

15

Heaven

Angela had continued her monitoring of Kaitlynn and Hattie's progress. Kaitlynn seemed okay and had her ducks in a row, so to speak. She appeared to at least have some idea as to what she wanted to do and where she wanted to go. But the other girl, Hattie, was really having a rough time of it.

Right now, Angela was extremely concerned with Hattie's problem with depression. She knew that Hattie wasn't handling it properly. Angela also knew that this was a time for Heaven's 'Hands Off' policy for any interference from Above.

Depression was, very often, or at least meant to be, a time of soul searching and spiritual growth. It was a very important function of being Human.

It was Angela's experience that some times the only time Human Beings do what they are suppose to be doing, learning about their inner selves, their spirituality, growing etc., is when they have what humans call 'set backs' or 'depression.' Many humans think that depression is the worse thing in the world, and it can be when one fails to grasp the reality of why and what is really happening to them.

In Heaven it was common knowledge that a depression was a good thing. It was usually the only time a human deeply and seriously communicated with God.

These depressions are very often, also, the best time to tap into one's creativity. Some of the best art, music, literature, poetry and major world contributions come from a depressed soul. Depression happens for a reason. It is meant for a time of contemplation and deep reflection. It mostly shows itself when a person has a major life change or is ready, and having trouble, entering a new life cycle. Unfortunately, it is often seen as a time of fear of the Unknown. Fear is actually the only real negative thing on Earth. A Human's fear or act of being fearful is the only real barrier to inner growth and/or happiness.

Some of life's cycles are birth, adolescence, leaving home, marriage, divorce, moving, job changes, illness and death of a loved one. Some people are able to flow smoothly through these kinds of changes with relatively little upset. Others experience heart wrenching pain and depression, usually because they tend to be resistant or fearful of any changes.

Angela had great empathy toward the earthlings. She knew the many obstacles and limitations that humans face on Earth. And because of the immense variety of problems Humans do face, she understood why God showed such great favor and love to the spirits who have chosen to 'do time' on Earth. They are the great explorers, inventors, authors, artists, musicians, teachers, doctors, engineers and livers of life. God is especially proud of those souls who volunteer to go to Earth. (We all choose our lives, believe it or not.) Sometimes God gives us a nudge to head in a certain direction and we tend to call these nudges our 'callings', but for the most part we do make the choices. We choose to live in poverty, or with sickness, or as a minority, or with handicaps. For these are the souls who truly bring the greatest joys and happiness to their fellow human beings who have been blessed with the mission to take care of them, love them and most of all, learn the important lessons from them.

Even the alcoholics, drug addicts, hookers and homeless hoboes hold a special place in God's Plan. If a human being can find compassion and love for some one in the dregs of life on Earth (man's perception, not God's) great and wonderful lessons are learned. So many people can benefit from the lessons of just one drunken man. One drunken man who stops traffic, vomits on the sidewalk, or leaves a family behind, touches every human being he bumps into. The affects can be good or bad. Depending on each individual's openness to a good or bad learning experience, will determine how and what a human gets out of this meeting with a drunken man.

Most humans have a difficult time seeing beyond the afflictions and angst of other humans. But then again, that is why they have chosen to go back to Earth; to try, try, try again to get beyond and master these important barriers to true spiritual growth.

Angela also knew that many of the more advanced spirits living on Earth are often the loneliest, homeliest and hardest people to be accepted by others. They are often considered the most troublesome people by their fellow earthlings. They are the ones that always seem to rock the boat. But Angela knew that in God's Plan the boat has to rock and sometimes even sink, before anyone can get to where we are all headed- to be rejoined with God in Oneness. (It sure has been a long ongoing, seemingly endless road…)

Angela knew that only God knows what the final out come will be. But her faith (and curiosity) was what kept her going. She was still learning, but it was considerably much easier where she was than where poor Hattie was. Angela was secretly grateful for that. She had learned her lessons well and earned her place in Heaven. But she still had a ways to go before she could go up to the next level. Angela had no idea when she could go up to the next level. There was no longer 'death' to signal time for the level change, like on Earth.

Things were quite different in Heaven.

16

Kaitlynn

1916

Kaitlynn, now 25, had made it to San Francisco, California. She had had a rough scene with her parents three years ago. It was practically unheard of for a single young woman to travel by herself. Even going into the local town was frowned upon let alone traveling cross-country. Terrible labels like 'prostitute' or 'loose woman' were whispered behind her parents back in their hometown of Plymouth, Massachusetts, when the town folk would talk about Kaitlynn and what she had done. Secretly, these folks were glad that their daughters were safely married and having babies. Their daughters had conformed to the society of the day.

Kaitlynn's trip cross-country was fairly uneventful. She had traveled through many of the great cities of the West, like St. Louis, Kansas City and Denver, and immensely enjoyed seeing all the different landscapes and the people inhabiting them. She had met many characters at the several train station stops and layover. She even got to see a few Indians at various stops along the way. (The Indians will be given citizenship of

America in 1924). They were quite civilized and she rather liked them. It was nothing like she had anticipated or pictured or heard about in her younger years. She had expected the train to be ambushed by Indian heathens and murderers. It didn't happen.

Kaitlynn's train had stopped in Kansas City for a six-hour lay over. In those six hours, Kaitlynn made a point to check out the city. She walked down many of the small side streets and window-shopped. After a while, being hungry, she stopped in a small diner. She desperately craved a good home cooked meal. Diners were known for their cheap prices and lots of good hearty food.

While in the diner, Kaitlynn saw a young lady who looked to be around 15 years old, sitting with another older woman, having a meal. The young lady and Kaitlynn caught each other looking at the other, and smiled. The mother, noticed that Kaitlynn was eating alone and invited her to join them. Kaitlynn happily obliged.

"Thank you so much for your kind invitation," said Kaitlynn grateful for the company. "My name is Kaitlynn Smith."

"Where are you from?" asked the young girl not recognizing Kaitlynn's New England accent. "Oh, my name is Amelia, and this is my mom, Mrs. Earhart."

Kaitlynn proceeded to tell them where she was traveling from, where she was going and even mentioned that she had wished that she could have flown coast to coast, as the train ride was dirty, slow and uncomfortable.

Amelia really perked up when she heard Kaitlynn mention flying. "I've always wanted to fly, too!" she explained with much animation.

It wasn't long before Kaitlynn and Amelia were in a very animated conversation talking about flying and how they had both felt after reading about the Orville and Wilbur Wright first flight at Kitty Hawk, North Carolina in 1903.

Kaitlynn was amused and enjoyed Amelia's enthusiasm as it reminded her of herself and her own dreams of flying some day.

Kaitlynn asked Amelia for her address and promised to write to her as soon as she was settled in California. They both were excited about having a new pen pal and a new friend with the same interests. They said their good byes and parted with the promise of hopefully flying together some day.

Kaitlynn had to hurry back to the train station so that she wouldn't miss her train.

Once Kaitlynn arrived in San Francisco, she managed to find a room at a woman's YWCA near the bay. It didn't take her long to settle in as she had very few personal belongings, but this was an advantage, especially since her room at the YWCA was quite tiny. She also found a job witnessing and doing dishes in a small cafe. It was a temporary job, as she had much bigger plans for her future.

She also immediately wrote a letter to Amelia Earhart. She told Amelia about the rest of her journey, about her room and about her new job. She also wrote more about her dreams of flying in the future. She wrote about the other men who have attempted and succeeded in building and flying better and better airplanes, that she had read about recently.

Kaitlynn just knew that one day she would fly. She might even fly with Amelia some day. She had never met another person who felt the same way she did about wanting to fly.

Kaitlynn continued to write occasionally . She knew that Amelia was about nine years younger than her, so would have to wait until Amelia had finished school before they could really make plans about really flying. Kaitlynn patiently told herself that the airplanes will probably be much better and safer then. She could wait.

In the mean time Kaitlynn found a new job at a local newspaper, the Hearst owned San Francisco Examiner. She was only a gofer and girl Friday, but her foot was in the door and she knew that she was now in a position of really being able to keep up on all the fascinating news and inventions and happenings that were occurring in the world around her.

She was now also able to find her own apartment in a boarding home where she was allowed to have a dog. She immediately went out and got herself a golden retriever she named "Flyer."

While she worked at the newspaper, she learned to type and mastered the skill rapidly. She soon was helping the reporters with typing their articles.

In Kaitlynn's spare time she got involved in the Woman's Suffragette Movement. She thought, as did her 'sisters', that women should have the right to vote. That was their main issue at this time. The Woman's Movement provided Kaitlynn with the companionship of other women who thought intently about their future and the future for all women. They wanted tomake life better and easier and more pleasant for women. They had all grown up with mothers who worked so very hard day in and day out and aged too, too quickly. As much as they admired and loved their mothers, they did not want the same kind of difficult life for themselves. They wanted the daily parts of their lives to be easier so that they, like men, had more time to explore, experiment, investigate and play in the world around them. There has to be more to life than cooking, cleaning and having babies and then you die.

But the suffragettes, the very first feminists, were having a hard time getting their messages out. The men did not want to give up any of their control and power to a woman. To these men, any woman who was not doing womanly things at home, was far from being an ideal woman. After all the bible tells them so . (And who do you suppose wrote the bible? Men.)

Well, the feminists of the early 1900's were probably more advanced spirits, ahead of their time. This world would prove to be an on going struggle for all older and more advanced souls throughout all time.

It seemed that anyone, male or female, but mostly female, who wanted to make changes, and for the most part, make things better for the masses, were often met with resistance. The resistance, however, usually made the doers and the shakers, fight all the harder for what they were striving for.

Eventually most things would change and it usually was for the better of mankind.

Kaitlynn often wondered why the common man or woman, struggled so hard against change. She loved changes.

17

Hattie

2006

Hattie had finally met a wonderful man. The way it happened was actually quite a fluke. She often sat back and marveled at her good fortune. It happened a couple of years ago.

She had just seen her therapist, as she was still trying to deal with the depression that had settled on her soul for several years, and was in the process of leaving the therapist's office. It had been a fairly upbeat session and Hattie was feeling pretty good for a change. For once she wasn't crying. Thinking about her session and her feelings of the moment, she wasn't paying much attention to her surroundings and where she was going. She bumped right into a man who was waiting for his session to begin. They literally bumped heads. Both apologized and asked the other if he/she was all right.

Their eyes met, a spark ignited, a conversation began and cell-phone numbers were exchanged.

The rest is history, as they say.

From that point, and after their Data-Diaries were approved by each of them, a short engagement ensued.

They were perfect for each other. Soon they married, much to the delight and relief of Hattie's parents.

Hattie, now 25, was pregnant with her first child. She was 8 and 1/2 months along, and happy as a clam. Her husband, Jared White, was so much like her. She was Mrs. Jared White. She loved that name. She loved him. She loved the baby inside her. She loved her life, finally.

Her depression had dissipated the moment she had bumped into Jared at her therapist's office. Go figure…

Jared, a few years older than Hattie, was of medium height, 5'10", fair complexion, thinning light brown hair and warm brown eyes, had had many of the same negative views about his life and the way the world was changing so fast. He longed for the good old days. His aspirations were not in sync with most of his peer group. He only wanted to earn a decent wage, have a pleasant home with a sweet and loving wife and lots of children. When he found out that Hattie wanted the same simple things, he fell head over heels in love with her. There was no turning back. So in a way they had been made for each other.

Hattie felt God's smile on their marriage. She felt truly blessed.

(She had also gotten the right baby, in case you were wondering.)

18

Heaven

Angela was pleased with herself. She liked the way she had finally been able to get Hattie and Jared together. Even her fellow angels gave her a pat on the wings and great kudos for her coup. It was a good match. But then again, it was part of Angela's job, to coordinate mates with each of her baby souls' time lines. It's just all part of the plan. As long as numbers weren't involved, Angela was near perfect at her job.

In spite of her earlier mistake of inverting years, both Kaitlynn and Hattie were finally adjusting and doing what they both had dreamed about as young girls. The council member had told Angela that life has a way of working itself out. It was part of God's Plan. But God was wise about not actually handing each soul's wish without some lesson or trial attached. It was a way to 'double-check' our real wants and desires. (Like They say, be careful of what you wish for, because we usually do get it at some point and in some form. We just don't always recognize that fact until much later in time.)

Kaitlynn was busy forging ahead with her futuristic plans of flying and making changes in women's lives, and at her own pace and with like-souls that she had traveled a great distance to meet.

Hattie had met the man of her dreams who wanted the same kind of life. So for now, all was right with the world.

19

Kaitlynn

1921

Kaitlynn was now 30 and quite settled and comfortable in San Francisco.

By this time the suffragettes had succeeded in advancing women's right to vote. They had won a small victory by securing this right , although, still with some limitations. They could now vote for a President of the United States, but there were still many restrictions and barriers regarding voting for every day issues and new laws and bills etc. But the suffragettes were a dedicated bunch and would continue to fight for equal rights.

Kaitlynn had also become a valued reporter for the San Franciscan Examiner. The Editor had given Kaitlynn her own by-line and column, "Women's Issues". Kaitlynn kept her readers informed on the suffragette's movement. Her column was often a source of controversy in San Francisco, but the nature of controversy is one of interest to many. And due to this factor the circulation of the Examiner steadily increased.

Kaitlynn had also maintained her volunteer work regarding the child labor problems. Some of the horror stories of the exploitation and abuse of young children in the work place were so horrendous that something had to be done to stop it. It also gave a good deal of fodder for Kaitlynn's newspaper column.

Many of her fellow suffragettes had joined Kaitlynn in this latest cause. They were beginning to make headway in getting new employment laws developed that would stop using children in such inhumane ways. Children should go to school and get an education before they have to earn a living, but if they have to work to help their families they should be treated decently and have a safe work environment.

The passion these young women gave to their causes was something to marvel at. This is the stuff dreams are made of. This is what gets things done. This is a perfect example of how God works, His plan and how He works through us.

In the midst of Kaitlynn's busy life, she had met a young man, Paul Taylor. There was a bit of romance happening between them. Although neither one was looking for a long term relationship or marriage. This was very 'New Age" thinking for the times, but then again, that's life and that's how time evolves and changes.

Neither Kaitlynn nor Paul cared much about what others think. It was, however, the early days of prohibition; the era called the Roaring Twenties. There was a lot of unorthodox goings- on at this time, all over the United States.

Kaitlynn eventually found herself with child. As independent as she was, she decided early in her pregnancy that she wanted this baby. Several of her sister suffragettes suggested that she get an abortion. The woman's movement had been working hard and diligently to put some safety and acceptability to what was and still is, a very deadly and secret and shameful operation. They felt that women should not be forced to be baby making machines, especially where many families could not support all the children they had. The suffragettes wanted to make abortion legal . (History would prove this problem to be on going.)

Kaitlynn was very surprised at the motherly instincts that kicked in as soon as she definitely knew she was pregnant. This didn't slow her down. She had big dreams about the wonderful life she and her child would have. She intended to bring her child everywhere she went.

Paul, pretty much went on about his own business. He had his eyes and aspirations on getting into politics. He had gone to Yale and gotten his law degree. He had grown up back east and like Kaitlynn, answered the inner call to go west.

Kaitlynn would happily become a single parent.

20

Hattie

2011

Hattie was very happy. She now had three children. Her first-born was a lovely daughter named Sonya. Sonya was now five years old and had proven herself to be a wonderful big sister to her two little brothers. Sonya was also very proficient at the use of the family's computer. It was amazing how smart kids were these days. Mastering the computer in the 21st century was as common as a child mastering the act of tying his own shoelaces in the 20th century.

Hattie's husband, Jared, managed an organic biosphere where much of their community of Plymouth, New Hampshire's food was grown. He was also involved in the genetic technology area. Most of the important medicines and drugs were developed in this same environment. Most of the world's drugs were now organic by nature with a mixture of certain herbs, minerals and other components, allowing for much safer medicines.

There were thousands of biospheres located throughout the world. These biospheres ranged in sizes from a few acres to several square miles, depending on location and needs of the area. Jared's was mid size and contained a miniature ocean, rain forest, grass land, marsh land, desert, a small farm, laboratories, work shops, education center and family recreation area.

In a biosphere every thing is recycled. Carbon dioxide exhaled by humans and small animals, birds, reptiles and insects, all living inside the biosphere, sustained the plant life and vice versa, the plants gave off oxygen for all the living creatures. Human and animal waste provided natural fertilizer for crops and fed the algae, bacteria and water plants that feed the fish. Electricity is generated by solar energy. The biospheres were necessary because there had been major, some severe, changes in the Earth's weather and climate. They provided a climate of moderation as there were fewer and fewer places on Earth that could claim a moderate climate. It was either too cold or too hot in most areas now. Over the past twenty years or so there had been hundreds of natural disasters, like major hurricanes and tornadoes, blizzards, volcanic eruptions, heat waves, flooding , forest fires, earth quakes, etc., and all the repercussions that resulted from such catastrophes. There had been a great loss of human and animal life as well as damage to the ecology in general. The biospheres became a viable alternative to try to maintain life in a controlled atmosphere.

Jared felt like a country farmer, which he loved. Even though the biosphere was high tech in its conception and operation, some one still had to plant, prune and harvest the products.

Although it was the 21st century, Hattie and Jared were doing old fashion, comfortable and peaceful things. Some how they had managed to find a simple life in modern times.

Hattie had calmed down considerably since she had married Jared and had three children. All the modern ways and major technical changes did not upset and confuse her like they did when she was younger and single. Having Jared by her side helped her to adjust. She even began to appreciate the convenience and ease that they're computer-controlled home provided.

With the push of a few command buttons, meals were prepared, house cleaning chores were robotically done, and for those who managed to still have some lawn outside, the grass was cut by a solar powered lawn mower. There was more time for a family to be a family, play games read or watch movies and television together. Even School was practically a thing of the past, most parents now a days self-taught their children at home. The computers were all inter-webbed and each student tuned in with other children and focused on a teacher located at the master site. Surprisingly, there was still a good deal of interaction between students as there were more field trips and more time for such excursions. Kids started their educations as soon as their parents thought they were ready, some earlier, some later.

As in Hattie's daughter, Sonya's case. She had shown intense interest in learning as early as two years old. Hattie and Jared encouraged her and Sonya spent most of her time at the computer learning and teaching her two younger brothers many of the things she was learning.

This allowed a good deal of free time for Hattie to catch up on her reading and self- reflecting. She remembered, years ago reading books about the many visitations that Mother Mary made in the 20th century. Mary had revealed many prophecies about the natural disasters that would affect the Earth in major ways. She had told several people that Humans had to change their ways. Even though there were still many small skirmishes through out the world there had been no major world wars. Most countries and their people were busy recovering after the devastation of life and property from the multiple natural disasters. As horrible as it sounds, these disasters were blessings in disguise. People had to tend to each other's basic needs and therefore, were becoming better people. Love and kindness were often the only commodities left to share with each other. Each country would help feed and clothe another country as they were able. In between each disaster the technology progressed at a greater faster pace.

As Hattie pondered all that had happened , just in the past ten years of her life, she marveled at the way everyone, including herself, was adapting to such a different way of living. Material things were not so important. For example, if a neighborhood was destroyed by a flood or storm or whatever, new condo-type habitats were built in place of single homes. All were equipped with the same modern conveniences, regardless of income. Every one had the same basics, period. Material objects were considered less important, because they could so easily be lost in a bad storm, fire, earthquake, etc. People were beginning to see craftsmanship, personal skills and professional services as the true priceless commodities. Beauty, wisdom, laughter and love were the things that really mattered. And this philosophy seemed to be spreading through out the world in 2011.

21

Heaven

Angela was soon to begin her new job. She had risen to a higher level of learning. It turned out that the dyslexic error she had made with Kaitlynn and Hattie had definitely turned out for the best. Just like the wise council member spirit had told her, "God works in mysterious ways."

Recently, there had been many natural disasters on Earth; earth quakes, volcano eruptions, floods, famine, droughts, epidemics, etc. Many new spirits had found their way to Heaven and were being assigned to many of the positions in the Birthday Center where Angela worked. These new arrivals had lived through some difficult times of late, and had learned many of the harder lessons on Earth, and so had rapidly risen to higher spiritual levels. Advancement was the name of the game. Spiritual Growth is where it's.

No one except God, knows how many levels there were, but each one seemed a fairly long haul, at first. Once a spirit rose to a new level, the atmosphere, the senses and the beauty was so much more spectacular than the previous level.

One would think that Heaven was, well, Heaven. But the differences in each level were awesome, intense and truly something to strive for, obtain and look forward to. Each level was so much better than the previous and more than one on a lower level could imagine.

Angela's new job consisted in arranging meetings with souls who had been in heaven for eons with recently arrived souls. Many were family members through out all of time, others were friends or people who had influenced each other some how, during their time on Earth. Where all spirits had different missions both in Heaven and on Earth, many lost track of each other. So it was Angela's job to reunite them.

It was a glorious and happy job to see two spirits greet each other after, what seemed to be, long periods of time. Heaven often seemed like one big happy reunion party. One might almost call Angela a reunion coordinator, a party caterer or the 'hostess with the mostest'. She loved her new position.

22

Kaitlynn

1926

Kaitlynn was now the proud mother of a gorgeous beautiful daughter, Alantra, who is now five years old. Alantra was adapting very well to her mother's busy life style. Kaitlynn had taught Alantra to read by three. Like her mom, Alantra had a voracious appetite to learn. Kaitlynn was now teaching Alantra some foreign languages such as French and Spanish. Alantra was proving to be a quick learner.

Alantra loved the hectic life her mother had introduced to her. Even when she was a small baby, she accompanied Kaitlynn to the suffragettes meetings, rallies and protests. She loved hearing the story that when she was a tiny baby, her mom would attach protest signs on the side of her baby carriage and march down the main streets with her. Alantra began her life as a feminist and would prove to be a great women's leader in the future. Another favorite story was while Kaitlynn was pregnant with Alantra, she had landed in jail for one night for picketing the California's Governor's office. Alantra really admired her mom.

Kaitlynn also took Alantra on their first airplane ride with Amelia Earhart. Amelia and Kaitlynn had maintained their friendship over the years and Amelia had even named her plane "Friendship" in Kaitlynn's honor. Amelia appreciated the way Kaitlynn had encouraged her on her pursuit to fly. Kaitlynn was one of Amelia's greatest fans.

Once Amelia had mastered the art of flying and purchased her own plane, she made it a point to fly to San Francisco to see Kaitlynn and Alantra. They took a short flight over the city and the beautiful San Francisco Bay. It was breath taking. Kaitlynn was ecstatic at finally realizing one of her first dreams. And the fact that she could share this moment with her daughter made it extra special. In fact, Alantra, was probably the youngest female to have ever flown so far.

By this time, Amelia had created quite a reputation for her flying feats. She told Kaitlynn about her plans to fly across the Atlantic Ocean by herself. This wouldn't happen until 1932, but Kaitlynn had no doubt that Amelia would do this.

Alantra loved hearing the stories that her mom had told her about Amelia Earhart. Her mom told her how she had met Amelia in Kansas City years ago while Kaitlynn was traveling cross country from Massachusetts to California. Kaitlynn and Amelia both had a yearning to fly as young girls. They had corresponded for several years as Kaitlynn, who was 9 years older, had to wait for Amelia to grow up. Kaitlynn always had faith that one of them would fly someday, it just happened that Amelia had had more opportunity and had access to planes first.

So by the time Kaitlynn and Amelia met each other again, Amelia had been a pilot for five years.

As much as Kaitlynn admired Amelia's accomplishments in flying, she knew that she wouldn't be able to actually learn to fly, especially now since she was a mother. The wanderlust to take unnecessary risks was down to a dull roar. She was quite satisfied to have just flown and now knew what flying high in the sky was like. It was wonderful. It was every thing she had dreamed about. She knew that flying would be and continue to be important to the future of the world.

Kaitlynn was very happy to let Amelia do the honors and receive the accolades and a renown reputation of being the first important and note worthy female pilot. Kaitlynn would chronicle her dear friend's progress in the San Francisco Examiner, where she was now a senior editor.

Over the years her column had been syndicated in most of the major newspapers through out all of the United States and Europe. Kaitlynn's popularity among her readers increased her stature in the newspaper world, and especially at the Examiner. It was still very unusual for a woman to hold such an important position in the newspaper business, or in any business for that matter. Both Kaitlynn and Amelia were considered very prominent and important women of their day. They both were flying high.

Women still did not have equal footing with men on voting rights. But that would change in 1928, for all women over 21.

23

Hattie

2016

After Hattie had her third child, she was unable to have any more. A new law had been past right after her youngest son was born, limiting off spring to three or less. It was a very unpopular law, but unfortunately it was now a necessary law.

The world's food supply, due to an unsafe environment and the dangerous toxic air quality, had dwindled to extremely low levels. Many major natural disasters had also damaged much of the prime farming lands through out the world.

The United States could no longer afford to feed the rest of the world. There was very little stored food in the nations coffers. If it wasn't for the thousands of biospheres that now produced 80% of America's food supply, things could be pretty dire. Therefore, family size had to be controlled.

Hattie would have liked more children, but now a days three children was considered a large family. So in that sense she did have the large happy family that she had always wanted.

Hattie's daughter Sonya, now ten, had proven herself to be bordering on brilliant in her self-education program. She was also a big help around the condo. Sometimes she was even tempted to have Sonya cloned.

Cloning was a new procedure that was quickly catching on nation wide. Although still in its early stages, the wealthy had been the only ones that could afford the procedure to either have themselves or a loved one cloned until now. (Computers started out like this before they became more affordable to the common man.)

The procedure began with an extensive scanning examination, which was done with a large piece of equipment that was a combination between a MRI screening and computer scanning machine. The scanning included a complete physical, genetic and intelligence scan of the real person. From the scanning a detailed computer program is created. This program could either be stored for future use, or immediately used to create a robot-like clone, identical to the person who goes through the procedure.

Outwardly the clone and person appeared to be the same, like a twin. But the clone was totally robotic- meaning it had absolutely zero feelings, it strictly obeyed orders and was used for assistance only. They were germ free, so far 'bug' free and could last forever.

One of the clones biggest use at this time, was in nursing homes and elderly center-condo-complexes.

There were now many more seniors in the world. The majority of the baby-boomers population were now all over the age of sixty-five and there were not enough younger people to take care of them all.

The clones in the nursing homes were mostly the children or younger relatives of the elderly patients. This way the elderly adult would always have a twin-member of their family, or a close friend or spouse, to stay at their side until the patient died.

This use of clones solved many of the serious and sad problems and conditions that plagued most nursing homes in the 20th century. Many of the elderly were suffering from Alzheimer's and dementia and other memory problems. So often these old timers were left to vegetate, sometimes for years, not ever seeing or knowing if they ever had visitors.

The clone acted as doctor, nurse and family member. Every senior patient was entitled to one as part of their retirement plan benefits.

The government realized that it would be cheaper in the long run to provide the clone- service for anyone who needed or wanted one, in place of paying wages to the hundreds of thousands of people it would take to take care of the growing elderly population.

Hattie recalled going to a nursing home with her parents to visit her father's mother. She was very upset at seeing her grandmother Rose, sitting in a room with several other elderly people doing nothing. They didn't talk or watch television or play cards. They just sat in that room day in and day out. It was a Special Care Unit for patients with memory problems. Many were also deaf and blind. There was nothing for them to do except sit- sit and wait to die.

It was so very sad. Hattie had wished that she could do something for these old people and especially for her grandmother. But her parents explained that there really wasn't any thing else they could do for her. Most of the time they would visit Hattie's grandmother, she didn't even know who they were. It made Hattie fearful of growing old.

"If only there had been clones back then," Hattie would think sadly, as she whimsically considered getting her daughter cloned.

Many hospitals today were also 90% cloned-staff. Very few humans were needed at these type of institutions. If humans were needed it was for maintenance of the clones or to purchase the medical, cleaning, laundry and food supplies needed to take care of the patients and manage the facility.

Clones were now also assigned to all handicapped or physically impaired persons. A clone of one's mom or dad, sister or brother, husband or wife, best friend or whoever, was made available to basically any one who needed assistance.

Once a clone was no longer needed or required, either because the person they had belong to died, or was able to be on their own again, the clone would be sent to a clearing house area. There they could be bought or sold like any other used appliance.

Many organizations would purchase these clones to help poorer countries, in ways similar to the old Peace Corps and VISTA programs.

Many used clones were purchased by N.A.S.A. who used them to man and maintain the space colonies that were now becoming more numerous, and to man inter-universal long range space exploration travels. Any where N.A.S.A deemed human life to be at too great a risk a clone would be substituted.

When the clone technology became capable of mass-production, there were many public protests and legal barriers incorporated to prevent exploitation and ill-legal use of clones. A large group of people were concerned that the clone would be used to create a superior army or be used to do evil things.

However, many precautions were set into place, such as particular computer chips that blocked all negative-type commands. A clone could not kill or endanger a human life in any way. A clone could not participate in any form of sexual activity or deviant behavior of any kind.. A clone could not destroy anything. So far, these computer chips have proven to be effective and tamper proof.

The world was becoming a nicer place, believe it or not. Most countries were too busy dealing with the basics of survival like feeding and housing their people. The huge number and magnitude of all the natural disasters that have been rampant over the past thirty years have kept human beings more concerned with survival than with disagreements over land,philosophy or idealism.

Hattie was grateful for the creation of clones, as both her parents were now living in senior centers, and their clones provided them with all of their necessities.

She visited by vision-phone almost daily, and they all got together on the holidays.

Hattie's daughter, Sonya, told her that she did not want to be cloned. Sonya was asserting her pre-adolescent individuality. Hattie agreed, but she was comforted by the knowledge that the clone option was available when and if it was ever needed.

Hattie and Jared were still blissfully happy with each other and their marriage. They were truly made for each other. (Angela's doing maybe??)

The whole family was happy and had become nature nuts. They spent most of their free time in the biosphere maintaining the crops and animals. The wonder of nature never ceased to amaze them. Secretly, Hattie hoped that nature would never be fully cloned.

24

Heaven

Angela was thriving in her new position of bringing old family and friend souls together again. These reunions were awesome to witness. It was so up lifting to her own soul to see the love and friendship rekindled.

"I love my job," she would sing. "If only this knowledge of always being connected to the ones we love was accepted by Humans while they are on Earth, the Earth would be a much happier place to be," Angela would think with some concern. She knew this to be a fact and true, now, and hoped and prayed that this knowledge would stay with her forever. "If Humans knew that this connection was for all time, maybe they wouldn't waste so much time clinging, possessing, obsessing, hanging on to someone who is dying, being fearful of life because they so fear death; if Humans knew this maybe then they would spend their time living, loving and learning. Life is suppose to be fairly simple, at least the everyday part. Yet Humans make every thing so hard and difficult," Angela sighed with empathy.

She remembered when she had first arrived in Heaven. Her mom, dad, aunts, uncles, cousins, great, great grandparents etc., were all gathered together to welcome her home. That's just what it felt like. It was as if she had been on a long, long trip and finally came home.

It was a glorious moment!!

Even though in Heaven every soul had tasks and lessons of their own to still learn and tend to, they only had to think of a loved one and that loved one would hear or know and respond in kind. The communication was all done through telepathy. One only had to 'think' about some one and that some one would pick up or tune in and great conversations took place without physically being together.

Angela loved this instant communication. She was also pleased to know and see that the Humans on Earth were constantly improving communication techniques and technology even with all the physical barriers. It had a long, long way to go, if it ever got there. (Again only God knows if and when mental telepathy will be available to Earthlings.)

Although many Humans do claim that they can intuitively communicate with some one that they are very close to, more Humans pooh-pooh the idea of intuition. If this wasn't so, more Humans would truly practice the Golden Rule-' do unto others as you would have them do unto you.' Because, intuitively, one knows if an action or comment is hurtful, either to another or to one's self. But does that knowledge stop a Human from hurting another Human? Sadly, not often enough.

It is possible, Angela surmised, that Humans did have the capability already, but just hadn't been able to really grasp or tap in to that part of themselves. There are so many distractions on Earth that seemed to keep Humans more disconnected than connected.

Angela hadn't forgotten about Kaitlynn or Hattie. They were still very much a part of her heavenly world. She was pleased that their lives were on track. She couldn't wait to reunite with them some day. She knew that this would definitely happen. In Heaven this was a given!

25

Kaitlynn

1931

Kaitlynn and Alantra had just gotten back to their apartment after voting in the local elections. Kaitlynn had played a major role in helping to secure the right to vote for all women over the age of twenty-one. Alantra's father, Paul Taylor, was now running for a seat in Congress. Of course, Kaitlynn and Alantra wanted Paul to win. Alantra was too young to vote, but she was well informed of the politics of the day, thanks to her mom, who was very involved in the local politics. Alantra still accompanied her mom every where.

Kaitlynn and Paul, although not married, maintained a great friendship and spent a lot of time together with Alantra, keeping alive a family unit. They often picnicked on the beach near the future site of the Golden Gate Bridge (which would be completed in 1937). From this lovely spot they could see Alcatraz Island where a huge fortress stood. It was a military prison, but from the beach it looked like a wonderful stone castle.

Kaitlynn and Paul shared many of the same visions and hopes for the future. At this point in time, they were both involved with trying to get birth control legalized. Kaitlynn had met Margaret Sanger a few years ago. Miss Sanger was involved with the Birth Control Clinical Research Center in New York City. She had been a major factor in getting the issue of birth control this far, although the clinic had been raided by the New York City police several times.

Right now the Federal Council of Churches was also a major player in the on going battle to protect women from unwanted pregnancies. Margaret Sanger had heard of the organized group of suffragettes in San Francisco and had traveled here to form a more united, nation wide coalition for Women's Rights.

Kaitlynn was thrilled to be a part of this now national movement. She gave this latest cause a great deal of press as she still wrote her newspaper column "Women's Issue" in the Examiner. Kaitlynn was also being sought out to speak publicly at various women's clubs, schools and organizations throughout the United States. She was paid handsomely for these speaking engagements, which also included traveling expenses for her and her daughter.

In other words, Kaitlynn was becoming a woman of substance and prominence.

Alantra loved traveling with her mother. She was getting an amazing education. Much better than if she had gone to regular schools. She was very proud of both her parents. Even though her family was very untraditional compared to many of her friends whose parents were married, she felt no negative stigmas. Actually the only people that seemed to have a problem with her mother's life style was her grand parents.

Kaitlynn had not been able to visit her folks much since she moved to San Francisco eighteen years ago. In fact, Kaitlynn had not visited them until fairly recently when the speaking engagements started. She had had a couple of engagements on the East coast over the past few years. Finally, Alantra was able to meet John and Mary Smith, her grandmother and grandfather. Alantra charmed them, but relations between them and her mom were quite cool. John and Mary were unable to relate or approve of Kaitlynn's single parent status. It was unacceptable to them and their religion.

Alantra would go to church with her grand parents when she and her mom were able to spend a few days in Plymouth, Massachusetts, but Kaitlynn never went with them. Alantra enjoyed the church experiences. She found the concept of religion quite interesting and took it upon herself to begin studying the different philosophies of the world.

Alantra and her mom had some heavy duty discussions about the different religions and their very different philosophies. Religion would be an on going interest to Alantra.

26

Hattie

2021

Hattie and Sonya were just getting home after a full day of shopping. They were looking for a prom dress for Sonya's first major dance.

Shopping was now a one stop affair. A mall was now almost as big as a city and totally enclosed. In fact, many of the smaller towns through out the United States had simply erected a bubble-type dome over the entire shopping and business district. The domes were designed to withstand the still on going onslaught of horrendous wind storms and erratic temperature changes. It was either too hot or too cold.

The individual shops and boutiques were all run by clones. Even the department and grocery stores were fully automated.

Humans still liked the idea of walking down isles and making their own selections of goods they wanted, even though almost everything including groceries, was available through mail order and televised home shopping shows.

A good deal of the food was now synthetic as were most beverages. Fresh vegetables and fruit and dairy products, and some meats, were still available thanks to the biospheres.

Drug stores were very busy places. Walking into one was similar to walking into an old fashion-type bazaar, or the fair-way in an amusement park. It was noisy with lots of people or clones set up in small kiosks offering free medical tests, giving self healing demonstrations, or physical make- overs with on the spot laser plastic surgery; psychics, channelers, therapists, masseuses offered immediate physical and mental relief. Various booths offered drugs that prevented or controlled obesity, stress, anxiety, and minor medical problems. There were pills now available for hibernation and vacation; for sex, fantasies and organ growth. The F.D.A., (Food and Drug Administration) approved almost any new drug, quickly, because if there was a problem it could be quickly corrected with another drug. It was definitely the era of 'quick-fixes'.

Humans now had more control of their health and well being than ever before.

There were drugs that improved memory and learning and drugs that controlled mental illness and senility. There were reliable drugs that controlled and/or alleviated fatigue, relaxation, alertness, moods, sleep, depression, personality, perception and concentration. These drugs had been so perfected that side effects , if any, were minimal.

At these drug stores complexes, people could also receive laser treatment for corrective vision, minor lesions and minor surgery.

The quality of life was one of good health for almost everyone.

There were still major diseases that continued to plague man kind like AIDS, Diabetes, Scleroderma, Lupus, Cancer, Arthritis, Multiple Sclerosis and variations of the above. There were also two more major epidemic diseases similar to AIDS that had come to the fore front at the turn of the century. The many natural disasters seemed to have awaken some old bacteria that had been dormant for many many years. So far the new diseases seemed to only affect anyone not living in dome covered areas and other poorer countries.

For the most part, people afflicted with long standing disease could self-medicate and often participated in helpful therapies that helped make their life more tolerable.

It was thought that most people born after 2011 would be born free of most genetic deficiencies and would grow up relatively disease free, due to all the advances in genetic technology treatment. Very few babies were born unhealthy. If a genetic defect was detected while the embryo was still in the womb, it could now be corrected, in most cases, prior to birth. If not, abortion was now a widely accepted alternative.

Hattie took great pleasure in knowing that her three children would live a long healthy and happy life. It was also a relief to Hattie to know that Euthanasia was also now an accepted option by an individual if medically needed. Physical pain and suffering were things of the past. People could now live relatively pain free even while afflicted with a major disease.

Hattie was excited and full of happy anticipation of the dance her daughter, Sonya, was getting ready to attend. Sonya had chosen a pink Mylar mini-tunic dress with matching pink sandals.

Most clothing today, was made of synthetic recyclable materials. Cottons, wool, furs, silks and other natural fibers were pretty much a thing of the past. Medical use was the exception for these products. The Earth could no longer support or sustain large herds of sheep, or any animal; or large plant crops, mostly because of the severe and destructive temperature changes. Cotton could be produced in small quantities in a biosphere, but not in the quantities that use to be produced back in the 19th and 20th centuries. Cotton was restricted for hygienic uses only, like sheets and towels.

The style of the day was very simple cuts like T-shirts, tunics, leggings, shorts; very basic but available in a large variety of bright colors. Color was still an important factor in fashion and color fads still come and go. There were no furs or leather clothing as all hunting of any type was banned.

There were lots of controlled zoos and aquariums through out the world which helped prevent, and kept extinction of the different species at bay. But wild animals were a thing of the past. Animals were treated with the utmost respect and the zoos and aquariums were very popular and visited often. To many going to a zoo or aquarium was like going to a church. It was a place of awe and reverence.

Most people had extensive CD-ROM libraries of wild life documentaries that could be viewed regularly in the comfort of one's home. Children loved watching these types of visuals.

Sonya's date for the dance was the son of one of the agriculture engineers who worked with her dad in the biosphere. His name was Kurt Kent. The dance was being held at the Education-Library Complex. The music of the day was all computerized. At teen dances, clones were used to hold guitars and play old drums just to give the dance a more exciting atmosphere. Rock and Roll, or a form of it, was still popular, especially the sounds of original rock'n roll that dated back as far as the 1960's. It was considered classical music to the teens of 2021.

Music was still a very important part of everyone's life, and so readily available in CD- ROM format that very few people felt the need to actually learn to play a real instrument. All one had to do was select the type of music one wanted to listen to and the type of instrument or

instruments that one wanted to hear, and one simply pushes a few computer buttons and Viola! So in that way one could be musically creative. There were also many, many museums located in the shopping complexes where any one could go to reminisce about old rock stars and bands. The Beatles were still considered the most popular group of all times.

Hattie and Jared were also very busy with their two sons, Jason and Justin, and sports. Although most sporting activities were done via virtual reality in large arenas, sports were still very exciting. Sports were now safer. There just were no more broken bones or black and blue injuries. One also didn't need to be of certain height, sex or strength to participate in any sport. Anyone could play any sport.

At the end of the 20th century most sport heroes and organizations became defunct. This came about due to the grossly over paid players and the overly high price of tickets to the sporting events. The sporting world priced itself out of business. The money involved and the greed that came with it became so obscene to the general public, that the fans revolted and ceased to go to the games and support the teams. Enough was enough. However, the yearning to compete was still a large part of human beings' make up. As a result of the ending of the sporting world as it was known throughout the 1900's, a large group of concerned citizens began an organization that decided to change the whole sport-industry. The people not only wanted to create something that was fun and exciting and something that anyone could participate in, but wanted to make it something that would no longer destroy self-esteem and egos by limiting sporting success to only those physically more accomplished.

Thus, virtual reality sports and arenas were established. This sporting form proved to be more popular and accepted than the old way of playing sports ever was. More people became interested in sports because now, more people, males and females, could now play them.

Ironically, the same thing happened in the film and entertainment field. The actors were paid too much, movies cost too much, both to produce and see. The public finally said 'No more!" Movie theaters were boycotted, actors were basically ignored and shunned. Finally,

Hollywood got the message. This also happened at the turn of the century. Movies, now, were all computer generated. Computer programs made it possible for anyone who wanted to, to make their own movie. One could also now put his or her own likeness via the computer, into any character role on the computer screen and really experience the theme of the movie. If there was someone one didn't particularly like, one could program that person into the part of the bad guy and watch him get blown up or whatever.

Psychologists later found that this computer control of this type of 'play' was very therapeutic. A person could safely act out his or hers aggressions or fantasies via the computer movie. As a result of this safe way to interact, there was less murder, less crime, less rape and less criminal activity, period. Another reason for the success of this computer usage, were the programs of accountability or repercussions to a person if they did commit a real crime. these programs seemed to really deter most people from stepping over the line.

Financially, life was evening out. If some people were wealthier now it was because they provided a good service or product. There was no longer outrageous overly paid sports or show business people. The proper moral priorities of who and what was of more value was finally in place and rightly so. People valued teachers, researchers, social workers, nurses far above lawyers, bankers, politicians, actors or athletes.

Wealth and too much money was considered an unwanted,(and not needed) burden by most ethical people. People learned and saw, by studying the history of the 20th century, how great wealth tended to create obscene abuses and sick greed of the rich people and those around that person. People could get away with murder if they had enough money. They would abuse their bodies and others with too much food, drink and drugs. They brought everyone down around them who had similar negative values, and, unfortunately most of society was headed to the sewer.

The want and lust of fame and fortune peaked at the turn of the century. Money was no longer the biggest consideration or motivation for a young person today when planning for future careers and goals. In fact, money ranked quite low on most everyone's 'want lists'. Even the money mentality changed in most big corporations. The big companies like the ones that built the biospheres, mall complexes, etc., put most of their profits back into their communities. This would enable just about every one to live equally as comfortable and as well off as their neighbors. This turn around in money-thinking came about as a result of the many natural disasters that had destroyed most of life and homes. No one had been left unscathed by these natural disasters. Total cities, towns and neighborhoods were ruined beyond repair. Most everyone had had to start from scratch at some point. Therefore, people pooled their individual resources and a form of equality emerged. There was no poverty or poor people in these renewed communities. Everyone's needs were the same now, as far as material things. People were happy to just have their family and friends and a roof over their heads as many had lost several loved ones and most had lost their homes in the various disasters over the years. Priorities were constantly changing for the better. All humans were benefiting, not just a few of what use to be considered the 'lucky ones'.

Sonya's prom and date was a success. Sonya and Kurt became great friends.

Hattie was pleased and content.

27

Heaven

Angela had just come from attending an intense reunion. Kaitlynn's mom and dad had been rejoined in Heaven. Kaitlynn's mother, Mary, had died three years ago (Earth time), of natural causes. Kaitlynn's dad, John, had died about six months after his wife's death. They say he died from a broken heart (actually it was a heart attack, but almost the same thing).

John and Mary were overwhelmed with joy at being together again.

Angela now had the daunting task of telling them about the mistake she had made a long time ago, regarding the mix up of Kaitlynn and Hattie.

Some how Angela had to explain that they had raised the wrong daughter. Technically, she knew that all's well that ends well, but she still felt that some kind of explanation was needed.

But before she confronted John and Mary, Angela needed to commune with one of God's council members. She wanted to handle this piece of information carefully and correctly, but she had some questions about how to do it.

Since Angela had risen to a higher level in the spiritual world, she wouldn't have to wait as long for a meeting with a council member.

The higher the spiritual level, the more knowledge a soul obtains. And because a soul has more knowledge, if there was a problem, it was considered to be a more serious problem. Therefore, a council member will make a point to handle the meeting request quicker.

Angela was summoned to the Council Hall. It was a crystal-like chamber that sparkled like millions of multi-faceted diamonds. It was absolutely beyond description, it was so glorious!

The wise spirit that spoke to Angela this time was a different one.

"What can we do for you, my child?" asked the spirit in a very soothing tone.

"I appeared before one of the other council members a while ago," Angela said a bit timidly.

"We remember," the spirit replied, "go on."

"Well, one of the mixed up soul's parents have arrived in Heaven. I feel that I owe them some kind of explanation."

"An explanation of what? For what?" asked the spirit.

"I thought that John and Mary Smith should know that they received Bob and Jennifer Jones' daughter and vice versa," said Angela nervously.

"We see," the spirit paused. "Why don't you tell us what you think you should tell John and Mary?"

"Okay." Angela had to think fast about how to put into words her mistake. "Um, well, gosh. My mind seems to be blank," she giggled with some embarrassment.

"Maybe that is your explanation," said the wise spirit.

Angela stopped and pondered what the spirit just said to her. Suddenly, she understood. "Yes, I see. I understand. By not explaining, there is no explanation. It is as it is suppose to be!" Angela exclaimed with delight.

"That is correct. It is God's Plan. Now go in peace and keep up the good work," said the wise spirit.

Angela practically skipped (if angels can skip?) back to her greeting station. She thought about the ramifications of what she just learned. If the mix up of Kaitlynn and Hattie is as it should be then it never really was a mix up. The two souls are living the lives they were meant to live.

"Wow!" thought Angela happily, "That's sure a load off my mind."

28

Kaitlynn

1936

Kaitlynn and Alantra had arrived back from the East Coast. Kaitlynn's dad had just died. The funeral was a sad affair especially because it was only six months prior that Kaitlynn had buried her mother. She hadn't gotten over her mother's death and now she had to deal with her father's death too. She and Alantra had even taken a side trip to New York City to take the elevator ride to the top of the Empire State Building to try to raise her spirit and get her mind off her sadness. Alantra had begged to go and Kaitlynn felt she owed her daughter this experience, although Kaitlynn's heart wasn't up to it.

Kaitlynn was suffering much guilt. She felt that she had abandoned her folks when she moved across the country to the opposite coast. She had only seen her parents a few times over the past twenty-three years. Remorse settled over her heart.

Her daughter, Alantra, had all she could do to comfort her mom. Alantra didn't feel too badly as she had hardly known her grandparents.

"At least Gram and Gramps are together again," said Alantra hopefully.

"You don't know that!" Kaitlynn snapped back.

"Don't you believe in Heaven?" asked Alantra.

"I don't know. Sometimes I do, I guess," sobbed Kaitlynn.

"Well, I do," said Alantra assertively. "I believe every one goes to Heaven."

"Maybe," Kaitlynn sighed as she went to her bedroom. She needed to rest. The two funerals in just a year's time was a lot for her to bear right now. (Not to mention how train travel is still too slow in Kaitlynn's mind. She wished that she and Alantra could have flown cross country. She just knew that travel by plane would some day be so much faster.)

Kaitlynn thought about the terrible argument she had had with her parents just before she moved to San Francisco . Her parents had never forgiven her for leaving them so far behind.

Kaitlynn felt bad that her parents would never be able to see or partake in her good fortune. Kaitlynn had become quite wealthy of late, due to the popularity of her newspaper column and all the speaking engagements she had had over the past several years.

Kaitlynn had just purchased a big new home on a lovely street, high above the beautiful San Francisco Bay. The view from their new home was stunning.

They were in the process of packing up the old apartment and were due to move in the new home by the end of the week.

Kaitlynn had also bought herself her first car, a Ford, of course. She loved the freedom she felt as she drove Alantra and herself around town and to and from work. For a single woman and parent, Kaitlynn's success was something to marvel at. She was definitely in a class by herself. Socially, her status presented a lot of problems. Single successful women were a rarity in this time period and society seemed to have a hard time handling it. Unfortunately, society tended to scorn women like Kaitlynn.

But Kaitlynn didn't let the negative attitudes of ignorant people get her down. she had her circle of friends and a wonderful career and a magnificent daughter.

Kaitlynn had promised Alantra a new dog once they moved into their new home. Kaitlynn's dog "Flyer" had died also, not too long ago of old age. It was time for a new one. 'Too bad parents couldn't be replaced as easily,' thought Kaitlynn wryly.

Kaitlynn continued thinking about her parents and hoped and prayed that they knew how sorry she was for the sadness she had caused them. She hoped that they'd know how much she loved them. Kaitlynn had faithfully mailed or wired money regularly to them to help them out. It was the least she could do. But deep in her heart she knew that it hadn't been enough to allay the pain. She knew that she had basically robbed them of their only grand child by living so far away. She prayed for their forgiveness.

Kaitlynn, however, went on with her life, but with a little less bounce in her walk.

She and Alantra moved into the big fifteen room house and busied themselves with decorating and painting. It helped keep her mind off her pain and sadness.

Kaitlynn was also looking forward to finding some time to read a new novel she had recently purchased, "Gone With The Wind". Reading had always been a form of escape for her.

29

Hattie

2026

Hattie and Jared were now in their mid forties. Physically, they were both in the best shape they had ever been in. With all the advances in health care, most people were able to maintain their weight, their physical agility and youthful appearance with great ease.

The hardest thing about this was that often times it was very difficult to tell the difference between the parents and their adult children.

Hattie's daughter, Sonya, now 20, had decided to go , and was now studying, at the Institution of Metaphysics and Spiritual Transition in Chicago, Illinois.

There had been major advances in the art of channeling , where spirits from the past could be contacted through a medium. The act of channeling had been dabbled with for years. Throughout history, many cultures had believed in and practiced similar ways to contact the dead. Channeling, in a big way, had started in earnest during the latter part of the 20th century. But only a few people back then, really believed or trusted in such feats of wonder. Back then, channelers, psychics, and New Agers were pooh-poohed and were often the brunt of jokes and scorn.

As is the nature of history, people tend to resist changes, new thoughts and ideas, but eventually truth and reality win out. Some things just take longer to prove it's validity. Superstitions and primitive religious beliefs have to be over come, and this is generally a slow process. But, people were beginning to open up and smarten up in the 21st century.

Sonya had become interested in channeling after having heard her mother, Hattie, talk constantly about a reoccurring dream of a woman living in the early years of the 20th century. Sonya was very curious to find out why the dream was on going and held Hattie in its grip.

Sonya was in the process of learning the newest relaxation techniques, through breathing exercises, yoga and meditation, in order to prepare and open her mind to receiving messages from the 'other side'. She was also taking classes in psychometrics, metempsychosis, parallel time tracks, teleportation, epistemology, levitation and mental telepathy. Sonya had opted on the ten year graduate program.

Most institutions of higher learning or colleges of the 21st century required six to fifteen years of study. There was no rush to hurry one's education these days, mostly because Humans were living longer and there was more time to dedicate to higher learning. The value of education had become extremely more important over the years. It was now appreciated more than ever.

The scientific community was very much involved in studying the connection of mind, soul and spirit. More and more miracles, near death experiences, visions of holy entities and ghosts had been occurring and reported since the turn of the century. So many more that scientists could no longer ignore them or write them off as flukes.

During one of Sonya's school breaks, she coaxed her mom into allowing herself to be channeled. Sonya had taught her mom some of the relaxation techniques that she had learned and was perfecting.

Sonya and Hattie had just finished thirty minutes of yoga exercises. Sonya told Hattie to lie down and close her eyes and concentrate on the woman that Hattie kept seeing in her dreams.

Sonya had darken the room, lit candles and incense and had American Indian flute music playing in the back ground.

"Are you relaxed, mom?" Sonya asked.

"Oh yes," murmured Hattie.

"Can you describe the woman in your dreams?" Sonya continued, "Picture the color of her hair."

"She has light hair," answered Hattie.

"How old is she?" asked Sonya.

"She looks like a young lady..in her teens maybe," Hattie went on.

"What is she doing?"

"Sweeping the floor in a small kitchen," explained Hattie.

"What is her name," asked Sonya, breathing deeply. She was preparing to call this girl's spirit into herself.

Hattie paused, "Kaitlynn. Her name is Kaitlynn." Hattie was feeling very excited once she mentioned the girl's name. She had always perked up, over the years, whenever she heard the name 'Kaitlynn'. She never knew why, until now, why that name interested her so much.

"Do you know what year it is?" asked Sonya.

"Early 1900's I think. Maybe late 1800's. I'm not sure."

"Mom," said Sonya, "I need you to be very quiet. Just keep the pictures of Kaitlynn in your mind's eye. It might take a few minutes before anything happens, so stay relaxed."

"Okay," replied Hattie.

Sonya closed her eyes and opened her mind by breathing and praying to Kaitlynn. "Kaitlynn, if you can hear my prayers please come to me."

Many minutes passed. The silence was very serene. Suddenly Sonya started shivering.

"I am Kaitlynn. I am here," Sonya said in not her voice.

Hattie's eyes popped wide open. She looked at her daughter who was sitting quietly looking at her.

"Who are you and why have you beckoned me here?" asked Kaitlynn/Sonya.

"I'm Hattie. I, ah..," she stuttered, "I dream about you a lot and I have wondered about you for a long time."

Kaitlynn, through Sonya, studied Hattie for a few moments, "We knew each other before," said Kaitlynn.

"Before?" asked Hattie. "Before, when?"

"In another place, " replied Kaitlynn. "In the spirit realm. In Heaven as you Humans refer to it."

"In Heaven?" Hattie asked in awe.

"Yes. We were born on the same day, May eleventh," Kaitlynn said matter of factly.

Hattie couldn't comprehend this, as the woman in her dreams was definitely of a different era. "How can this be?" Hattie asked.

"You'll understand one day," Kaitlynn said as she slowly left Sonya's body.

Hattie saw Sonya collapse. She quickly got up and shook her daughter. "Sonya, are you all right?"

Sonya opened her eyes and took some deep breaths. "I'm fine," she said nonchalantly. "What happened?" she asked. When one truly channels, the in coming spirit takes over the channelers body and mind, so Sonya couldn't remember.

"Well, I do think Kaitlynn was here. She told me that we had met in another place," Hattie paused, then quietly said, "She said we met in Heaven."

"Wow!" said Sonya. "It worked! My professor will be so proud of me." Sonya seemed more interested in her accomplishment than in her mother's profound experience. Sonya had taped the encounter as she needed to write a report on her success. She quickly grabbed the tape recorder, hugged her mom, and went directly to her bedroom, leaving behind a stunned and confused Hattie.

30

Heaven

Angela was in the process of learning another interesting phase to her position of Reunion Coordinator.

As she continued monitoring Kaitlynn's and Hattie's life on Earth, she was pleased to notice that Humans were becoming more efficient with the use of their brains. Many were learning to trust their intuitions and inner voices. Some had learn to tap into the brain's capability of seeing beyond their physical existence.

Angela could see, and with great pleasure, that the Human Being was finally evolving into more positive and more aware beings. Many were learning, and accepting, that the universe was much bigger than just themselves.

There appeared to be more praying, requesting of assistance for good things and the desire to continue communication with people who had left Earth's reality. The Earthlings seemed to need, and wanted, contact with dead family and friends, to either make amends of past wrongs done to them when they were alive or to find out if they were now pain free, especially if the dead one had died a painful death through an accident or debilitating disease.

"Better late than never," thought Angela.

It was part of Angela's job as a liaison spirit, to send signs or messages from her now fellow spirits (If God directed her to do so), to the people on Earth who desperately needed to feel some kind of on going connection. When a sign or message was received by a Human on Earth, many other people would tell the receiver of such a sign or message, that it was just a coincidence. There were still a lot of non-believers.

But the people who did receive a sign from Above, knew it, believed it and it very often changed and redirected their life for the better and the affect was usually forever.

Angela noticed, however, that not all requests were answered. God, or one of the council members, had the final say on all requests. She didn't quite know how the final determination was made. Why some Human's prayers were answered and others had to ask and ask and never got what they asked for.

She hadn't reached the spiritual level that allowed her to be privy to the reasoning behind, what appeared to her, to be the selective answering of prayers. Some spirits, hearing the prayers, went directly to God to ask if they could 'visit' a loved one still on Earth.

Angela guessed that it must depend on the urgency, importance or sincerity of each individual request.

Angela did know how frivolous Humans could be with their requests. Some wanted more money for things, some prayed to pass some kind of test, some prayed to get out of the trouble they put themselves in etc., etc. Too many people prayed for the wrong things or for a short cut out of pain and turmoil. Humans mistakenly thought that they could use prayer an God to save them from punishment or suffering. 'We are all accountable for our own sins.' It seemed too many Humans thought otherwise or were being misled by misinformed, badly directed, selfish religious leaders.

She figured out that many prayers were unanswered because a Human had to learn something from what ever event or situation they were praying to solve or get out of. This did make some sense to her. As Angela thought about all this, she felt some relief that she only had to do God's bidding and that she did not have to make all the major discriminating decisions that were constantly put on His shoulders every moment of every day. The enormity of God's responsibility was practically incomprehensible, not only to Humans, but to Angela too.

Angela had been hearing Kaitlynn's prayers of late. She knew that Kaitlynn wanted and needed forgiveness from her recently departed parents. Angela felt bad for Kaitlynn. She still felt some responsibility for Kaitlynn's and Hattie's problems. She thought that if she hadn't messed up way back when, Kaitlynn may never have needed to move so far away from her parents, and hurt her parents so badly in the process.

Angela decided that perhaps she could go to God directly and intervene for Kaitlynn so that Kaitlynn could find some solace and feel forgiven. She was sternly told by one of God's council members, that " It would be handled in due time." (What ever that meant.)

31

Kaitlynn

1941

Kaitlynn had begun to slow down some. Not because she wanted to, but her body just couldn't keep up. She had seen a few doctors off and on over the past couple of years, but none of them could pin point or diagnose anything in particular. For the most part, she was told that she was getting older and older people have to slow down. One of the doctors gave her a tonic that was suppose to help. It was a mixture of cod liver oil and some vitamins. Kaitlynn took it daily, but it really didn't seem to help much.

She also missed her daughter Alantra. For some unknown reason to Kaitlynn, Alantra had decided to become a Catholic nun. A nursing nun to be exact. Kaitlynn and Alantra had had many arguments over this life choice that took Kaitlynn by surprise.

Her daughter had always had an interest in religion and had studied philosophy and sociology her whole life. Whenever Alantra went to a library with her mother, she would gravitate to the religion section. Children's books were of little interest to Alantra, even as a young child.

She preferred stories about Jesus, Buddha, Saint Teresa and other religious persons.

Kaitlynn just didn't think that it would end up with Alantra giving up all the wonderful things that Kaitlynn had worked so hard for her whole life to give Alantra so that she could have a better life.

Kaitlynn often blamed herself for Alantra's abrupt about face. She had taken her daughter to all her speaking engagements all over the United States and Europe. Alantra had participated in many demonstrations and protests with her. They had even flown together. Maybe she had given Alantra too many exciting experiences, that Alantra now craved a quieter, more peaceful life.

The one major similarity between Kaitlynn and Alantra was the common bond of wanting to live with and for women. They had put women's issues and rights above all else.

Kaitlynn supposed that that was a good thing. "At least it isn't a cloistered convent," Kaitlynn thought with a sigh.

Kaitlynn had begun to limit the number of speaking engagements to only a half dozen or so a year. She just didn't have the stamina any more for all the traveling that it entailed.

She had even hired herself a personal assistant to type her newspaper column that she still wrote for the San Francisco Examiner. Kaitlynn had noticed that her hands were often very stiff and swollen in the mornings. The skin even seemed tough and she couldn't move or use her hands the way she use to. Typing had become near impossible, so she had resorted to dictation.

At least her mind still functioned as clear as ever. For that she was grateful.

She had lived at such a hectic pace for so many years that all that expended energy was finally taking its toll on her body.

It was frustrating to Kaitlynn to sense and know that something was wrong, yet no one could tell her what was going on with her body. The closest she got to getting any kind of answer was that one doctor said it might be arthritis. Well, she figured she could live with that, as long as she had some assistance. "After all," she thought, "I am fifty years old."

Kaitlynn didn't let herself wallow too long in self pity. There were too many other serious things happening in the world around her. She, as was the rest of the citizens of the United States, was concerned about the bombing of Pearl Harbor in Hawaii, by the Japanese. World War II was raging in Europe and Russia and now the Philippines and Japan were involved. There had been disturbing reports coming in to the newspaper almost daily by the Associated Press, about some horrible atrocities happening in Germany and Austria. It seems that the German dictator, Hitler, was literally exterminating as many Jewish, Slavs, Gypsies, homosexuals, and political enemies as he could. There were horrendous stories heard on the radio about concentration camps and gas ovens and unspeakable experiments that the Germans were doing to the millions of victims of Hitler's hatred.

It was incomprehensible to Kaitlynn that such atrocities could actually happen in this world. She took it upon herself to use her column to rile and incense her readers to do something, to get involved any way they could to help America stop this awful war.

Thousands of women went to work in the factories and hospitals as their husbands, brothers and fathers joined the military to help stop Hitler and now Japan.

Kaitlynn and the suffragettes helped with special blood, bandages and metal drives. They collected any thing and every thing they could that could possibly help their soldiers and country.

Because of Kaitlynn's physical impediments, she found herself more in the back ground acting as a great motivator. Through her newspaper column and local public speeches she was able to encourage more and more people, especially the women, to get involved any way they could.

Kaitlynn even received a commendation from President Franklin D. Roosevelt for her contributions to the war effort.

Kaitlynn, knowing that her daughter was safe, went on about her business as best she could. One of her newer local causes which came about as a direct result of the bombing of Pearl Harbor, was the sudden anti-Japanese stand the United States government was taking on all American-Japanese people. The U.S. government was rounding them up and herding them into prison camps, thinking that they were now traitors to America. Kaitlynn and her group were protesting this act claiming that it made America look as evil as Hitler and Germany. However, her protests seemed to go unheard as it seemed the majority of Americans at that time, were too fearful of becoming directly involved in World War II and didn't trust any one or anything except their own government. Kaitlynn's work, although not immediately appreciated, would help to establish the future organization of the Universal Declaration of Humans Rights that would eventually protect all American citizens of their civil and political rights. These rights would include the right to life, liberty, education, religion, nationality, association and information.

32

Hattie

2031

Hattie and Jared now had their condo to themselves. All three of their children were grown and out on their own, away at various institutions of higher learning. Both of their sons, Jason and Justin, were studying to become space explorers and astronauts.

There were now, several established space colony-laboratories. These space colonies had proven to be safe and successful and were now in the process of recruiting new and younger astronauts. Prior to this, mostly clones and experienced older astronauts, manned and operated the space stations. There was even a large space colony, or lunar settlement, now located on the moon.

Many experiments were being conducted to try to control the weather on Earth. The Earth was still experiencing very erratic and extreme weather conditions. Particularly the hurricanes and wind storms in general were creating massive natural disasters. It was thought that these storms were the result of the extreme hot and cold temperatures that came about as the Earth's position and rotation had been steadily shifting and tilting differently. The scientific community had been trying to figure out why this was occurring. Henceforth, the space colonies had been developed out of an urgent necessity. From the space colonies, the Gulf Stream could be observed, and its lack of steady patterns proved to be one of the reasons for the continuing weather-havoc on Earth.

The scientists thought that if they could find a way to harness the energy of the Gulf Stream, they would then be better able to control and direct the energy of it, and begin to ease up some of the physical destruction and the devastation of its people, that had been on going since the end of the 1990's.

Although, most people were now protected under the bubble-type domes that covered the biospheres, condo complexes, all shopping and city areas, there was still great concern that if the rest of the unprotected land masses were not protected, the earth would become totally barren like the moon and the other planets in the immediate universe.

Hattie was proud of her sons' patriotism by wanting to go into space and help save the planet Earth.

She was, also, very happy with her daughter, Sonya's, progress in her chosen metaphysical field. Sonya had become very adept at channeling, levitation and mental telepathy. These skills were becoming widely accepted as an important tool to help Humans understand life and death, and live happier and fuller lives. This was accomplished by the removal of fears of , what once was considered, the unknown. Human intelligence was growing and expanding its views by leaps and bounds, as was the technology.

Every day life was so much easier now, regarding daily maintenance and hygienic tasks. Every one had a better quality of life and had much more spare time than ever before. Humans were now able to devote the majority of their time to their families and creative pursuits. Much time was now spent on soul-searching and one's spirituality growth.

People on Earth were more peaceful and loving, not only of themselves, but of others also.

As isolated as life appeared to be on the outside because of all the seclusion-like domes separating towns and cities and countries from each other, there was actually more heart felt communication going on. Communication was readily available, and very inexpensive, via one's wrist cell phone, or through the internet on the computers. Also, now that more and more Humans were beginning to use more and more of their brains and the art of mental telepathy was becoming easier and easier to perfect, there was more communication via thought-waves (which didn't cost a thing!)

People were now so involved with expanding their minds that there was very little thought given to material things. Few people coveted or envied the 'things' of others. Every one pretty much had every thing that was needed, and the pleasure one now got exploring their own minds , took up most of the time a human use to spend on accumulating things.

What use to be considered 'extras' like Jacuzzis, computers, fancy cars, stylish clothes, jewelry and cash were either a given, or not needed, or no longer made and available. Every one had computers, combined with entertainment centers. All condos were built with great bathrooms, although water usage was carefully monitored. There was no individual ownership of personal cars, yet transportation was readily available in every community where needed, as fuel was rationed due to the dwindling of natural resources. Most vehicles were electric or solar and technically owned by each community and therefore, available to every one. Air transport was the norm and the preferred means of travel between cities and countries. For short trips, the hover plane or helicopter was used. The multiple natural disasters had made land travel, thus automobile travel, very unsafe, as most interstate highways and roads had been washed out or destroyed by floods and earth quakes, etc. The government had stopped rebuilding the main roads because another natural disaster would take it out and it became a huge waste of government funds, so most people took to the air.

One only had to go to their local biosphere, zoo or aquarium if they wanted to commune with nature.

Things were definitely different now, but life, believe it or not, was actually much better.

Hattie and Sonya regularly communed with Kaitlynn, especially since Sonya had perfected the knack of channeling.

Hattie had learned of Kaitlynn's dreams of flying and all about her move to San Francisco in the early 1900's. It was like studying history lessons on a first hand basis. Hattie and Kaitlynn were becoming great friends through their channeling experiences.

Hattie also, shared her life with Kaitlynn, and told her how she had wished she could have lived in Kaitlynn's time. Kaitlynn told Hattie how she always knew that flying and landing on the moon would one day happen. Hattie often wondered what it would have been like to have lived Kaitlynn's life. But, in a way, she was…

33

Heaven

Angela had recently returned to Earth at God's direct request. There had been a young child lost in Yosemite National Park in California. God had instructed Angela to find the child and lead him to safety. Angela found the young boy cold, wet and shivering by a water fall about ten miles from the campground where his family was frantically searching for him.

This was an example of God's answering someone's sincere desperate prayers. Not to mention that the young boy had much work to do while on earth, and it was not his time to die yet. Periodically, God would send one of his millions of angels to Earth to assist in restoring someone's life back on to the right path, literally. Many of these types of interventions go unheeded as help from above, and are only accepted as fortunate luck.

The little boy only remembered meeting a young woman near the water fall. The young woman had 'been hiking' and realized that once she came upon the boy that he was lost. He was able to tell the young woman the name of the camp ground where he had been camping in with his mom and dad. The young woman, 'knowing where the campground was', brought the little boy back to safety.

As his parents hugged him with all their might, amidst a crowd of people who had also been searching for him, the young woman who had brought him back in to the camp ground, just seemed to ' fade away' into the background.

In the family's frantic, joyful and emotional reunion, they forgot to thank the young woman for her help. The little boy kept telling his parents that the young woman was an Angel.

"Of course she was," said his mom placatingly," she saved you." All the while she thanked God and wondered if the young woman truly was an angel.

Angela felt so blessed that God had made such a personal request of her. Being an angel, in any capacity, was truly the most wonderful honor.

Divine Intervention was another wonderful thing. It made Angela think about a television show on Earth that she and many other angels had heard about, which has created quite a pleasant hubbub in Heaven. The television show was called "Touch by an Angel". This television show was definitely inspired directly by God. Angela was convinced of this. This Human show delivered wonderful stories and information about how Heaven operated, in an entertaining round-about-way. Many angels had been directed by God to relate certain story lines to the writers of the show.

So many Humans chose the Hard Road. They learned things through horrendous situations. Everyone had 'their story.' No one was left completely unscathed by pain and difficult lessons, but it was how one came back from the hells they put themselves in, that was the true test. As long as the lessons were learned, it was a Human's choice to make which roads they would take.

God sent Humans so many messages in so many subtle ways. Some Humans knew and learned and abided by the Heavenly signs. But, unfortunately, too many Humans lived their lives oblivious of the many signs and miracles that happened daily around them.

God often sent an Angel to Earth to do something as simple as knocking a certain book off a shelf in a library or book store, in front of someone searching for guidance or needing an answer to either a conscious or subconscious problem. Or God would instruct an Angel to "suggest" that someone take a different route and He spared that 'saved' person from an accident. Some times He sent two Angels to guide two Humans to meet each other, for whatever reasons. And there was always a reason. But, Human nature being as it is, sometimes it took many repeat ' nudges' form Above before a Human did or chose to do what he or she needed to be doing.

Angela hoped and prayed continually that more and more Humans would learn to recognize all the favors and blessings God sent freely their way. Everyone received gifts from God, be it one's children, one's lot in life, one's good fortune, one's good health etc., etc. But sadly, too many people wanted more. They wanted to win the lottery or wanted to look like a model or a movie star, or wanted a more perfect son or daughter, or better parents, or a different nationality.. the list went on and on selfishly. Some of God's most impoverished people have the greatest abundance of Earthly love with their families, where as the wealthiest people wouldn't know love if they walked into it. Some of God's most handicapped people are the happiest and the most athletic are as miserable as can be. There is no rhyme or reason, no black and white, the grass is not greener on the other side of the fence. It is all right there within everyone's reach, one only had to reach for the right things, which can be different for everyone. It all comes down to letting go of the Fear and learning to Love unconditionally.

34

Kaitlynn

1946

Kaitlynn's health was deteriorating. Not fast, but slowly. she was finding it harder and harder to manage her once busy hectic life style. Her boss at the newspaper let her work and write in her own home. With the aid of a personal assistant, Tanya, who not only served as Kaitlynn's aide, but also was Kaitlynn's typist, house keeper, nurse and courier, Kaitlynn was able to maintain her job as an editor and a columnist with the San Francisco Examiner.

Her personal assistant became Kaitlynn's liaison to the outside world.

Sometimes Kaitlynn wondered how she ever functioned before Tanya came into her life. Especially since Alantra had left home. It kind of made her understand better how her now deceased parents felt after she had left home.

Tanya, Kaitlynn's girl Friday, was also Kaitlynn's main confidante. Fortunately for Kaitlynn, Tanya also believed in Women's Rights. They spent hours discussing the problems women faced in America and the world.

In many ways, Tanya's life mirrored Kaitlynn's. Tanya had left her home in the East to follow her dreams and also ended up in San Francisco. However, Tanya's childhood circumstances were much different from Kaitlynn's. Tanya had been a victim of child abuse, incest and molestation, at the hands of her father. Perhaps Tanya's reasons to go West were better than Kaitlynn's reasons.

Tanya was only a few years older than Kaitlynn's daughter Alantra. So in many ways Kaitlynn felt motherly towards Tanya.

At the moment, Tanya was pregnant and not married. Kaitlynn had no problem with that as she had also been an unwed mother. She had already opened her heart and home to Tanya. Kaitlynn was actually looking forward to having a baby in the house. Since she would never have grand children, Tanya's child would be the next best thing. Kaitlynn never asked about the father of Tanya's unborn baby, although she was aware of the girl's sad background.

Kaitlynn needed weekly enemas as her body had stopped functioning normally. She was also having a hard time eating most solid foods as her esophagus was almost closed up.

Swallowing was extremely painful and difficult, so Tanya would have to puree most of Kaitlynn's meals. They often joked about this as training for Tanya before her baby arrived.

But in spite of Kaitlynn's illness, her spirits remained high and positive due to the pleasant amiable relationship she had with her personal assistant.

Alantra made a point of visiting her now ailing mother as often as she could. Being a nurse and nun made her visits much easier, as she knew how to take care of her mother's special needs. Having a nursing degree, Alantra had been trying to research her mother's condition. She discussed her mother's many symptoms with several doctors. One doctor thought that her mother may possibly have a disease called scleroderma. Unfortunately, this disease was quite rare and not widely known about.

There was no cure as there was no known cause for it. The doctor instructed Alantra that all she could do was see that her mom was as comfortable as possible. The doctor also told Alantra that her mother could possibly live another ten to twenty years or she could die in six months. There was no real clear cut way to diagnose and treat scleroderma at this time.

Alantra did not tell her mother every thing that the doctor had told her. She just made sure that Kaitlynn got what ever she needed and wanted. Fortunately, her mother was very well off and could afford almost anything she needed.

As sick as Kaitlynn was, there were some days when the pain and fatigue were fairly minimal and on those days, Kaitlynn could accomplish quite a bit. She learned to take full advantage of the good days. Occasionally, the good days would stretch in to weeks. When Kaitlynn had some good weeks, she would make a point to schedule some speaking engagements and rallies for what ever cause was on the front burner at that particular time. However, the bad days were really bad. The pain could be horrendous and brutal. When these painful bouts occurred, Tanya or Alantra, would take Kaitlynn to the nearest hospital where she would be given morphine to ease the pain.

At home, Kaitlynn was ministered with codeine, a milder form of morphine, which Alantra was readily able to provide for Kaitlynn. Unfortunately, Kaitlynn was becoming more and more dependent on the codeine. She was probably becoming addicted to it, although back then, even doctors weren't as aware of the dangers of drug addictions.

Alantra had mixed feelings about her mom's dependency on codeine. One part of her thought that the addiction was better than suffering with the pain. She truly believed that people stricken with horrible diseases had enough problems to deal with without suffering the terrible pain on top of every thing else. There just weren't too many other choices back then. Alantra did her best to monitor her mom's usage of the codeine. That's all Alantra could do.

Kaitlynn knew also, that she was becoming very dependent on the drug and did her best to not abuse it. Many times she would skip her scheduled codeine doses and suffer the consequences, mostly so that she could be some what clear headed so that she could continue to write. She wasn't ready to succumb to the ravages of scleroderma yet. She still had a lot of work to do. She hoped some day to write a book about her life and was in the process of getting her diaries and notes together for that purpose.

35

Hattie

2036

Hattie, Jared, Sonya, Jason and Justin sat in the front row at the local funeral parlor, listening to a memorial service for Hattie's parents. Bob and Jennifer Jones had opted to die together in a joint pact that they had agreed to and had witnessed to, two years ago. They had decided that once either or both of them got too sick or too old, that they would die together.

Now a days, euthanasia, death by choice, was the main option for death, instead of being kept alive for years and years on all of the life-support machines that were available in all hospitals. Both of Hattie's parents had suffered strokes while living in a self-contained senior center, or what use to be known as nursing homes. At this point in time, once a senior citizen's health begins to fail, they are sent to a Senior Center. While there, they can opt for many mechanical devices that were now able to substitute for human organs, senses and limbs. They also could choose between natural death, euthanasia, or 'endless' life support. All corpses were cremated, although some people left instructions in their wills to be frozen by a technique called cryonics. Cryonics was a procedure that started in the 20th century as some people believed that after years of being frozen, they would be able to be brought back to life at a later date. So far this had proven not to work, but some still thought that some day it would work. At any rate, fire or ice were the only two options after death for the disposal of human remains.

It was widely accepted that we as Humans, could now choose how and when we die.

On the other end of the scale, women could now choose exactly how and when one wanted a baby. They could choose the sex of the baby, how they wanted to conceive, either naturally, by test tube or via a surrogate. Even though there was a limit on the number of children a woman could have, (three maximum), medical innovations had so perfected the act of conception that there were no longer any unwanted children, therefore only very few adoptions or abortions occurred.

As Hattie sat at her parents' funeral, she reminisced about how much her world had changes since 1981. She felt sad about the death of both her mother and father, but she completely understood and approved of their decision to go to the other side together.

Since her daughter, Sonya, had completed her education in Metaphysics, Hattie had learned and had a greater understanding and a stronger belief about life after death. Hattie also truly believed that she would see her parents again. Her experience with having 'met and communicated' with her spirit-friend, Kaitlynn, had proven to her that there was indeed more to life than just the time one spent on Earth.

Hattie also knew that now, with the help from her daughter's expertise in channeling, she would have many opportunities to continue to communicate with her parents.

Sonya was doing extremely well in her new profession, as a Doctor of Epistomology and Transpirituology. She had become widely respected and sought after. Humans were readily adapting to the belief of life after death in droves, forcing Sonya to hire more and more staff and fellow doctors in her field. They could barely keep up with the demand for their services.

When Sonya did find some spare time, she would visit her mother and tell her mom about all the interesting people and their lives, past and present, that she was meeting and learning about. She also told Hattie that she had been in contact with an angel named Angela. Sonya was so excited that she had actually made contact with a real Angel! She told her mom that she and Angela were becoming good friends and that , in a way, they had similar jobs. Sonya reunited people on Earth, and Angela reunited people in Heaven.

Hattie had no doubt that Sonya was telling her the truth. How could she not, after having her own personal experience with meeting Kaitlynn?

Hattie was spending a great deal of her time with Jared in the biosphere. She had become an excellent gardener over the years. She felt a wonderful sense of peace while working with plant life.

With all the new modern rejuvenation techniques now available, both Jared and Hattie were able to maintain good healthy youthful lives. She and Jared also had many intense, deep conversations about their daughter's profession and accomplishments regarding the spiritual realm. Jared wasn't quite as open or susceptible to the beliefs of life after death, but with age, he was becoming more open minded about some of it. He was more interested in his two sons', Jason and Justin, escapades in outer space. Neither Hattie or Jared had seen them for several years, as the boys were on twenty year tour of duties. However, they were in regular contact with them. Hattie and Jared loved hearing about their experiences living in the space colonies and their many inter-planetary travels.

Because of the advances in telecommunications, they were able to receive live picture and conversations through their television in the comfort of their media-living room. They felt very much a part of their sons' lives and a part of the space colonies. Information from all over the world, and now the universe, was amazingly instantaneous.

36

Heaven

Angela was having a ball communicating with people on Earth, especially with her new friend, Sonya, and a few others who had highly developed their communication skills with the spirit world.

She was so pleased that Humans had finally been able to break through the mind barrier and make the connection. She was particularly pleased that one of the connections had come from Hattie's daughter Sonya.

Unlike some spirits, angels could only connect directly. In other words, Angela could not directly communicate with Hattie unless Hattie could develop the skill herself, which, unfortunately was unlikely due to Hattie's age and limited education level.

This kind of connection was different than the channeling process, where an Earthling, through the help of a third party, could 'meet' with a deceased friend or family member. (Don't ask me why it's different, it just is.)

Supposedly, Angels were on a higher spiritual level than the recently arrived souls of the past several hundred years or so. Any one still on Earth who had a strong desire and need to 'meet' with an Earth departed loved one, could, if they truly believed, communicate with the dead, if they practiced the skill. There were also, now places where Humans could retreat to, called pschomantrium inns. One could rent a room that was dark and mirrored, and with some concentration call forth visions and or visits from departed spirits. This technique was developed by a Dr. Raymond Moody in the 1990's. It was considered kind of a crude method, by today's standards, but Angela remembered how excited they all were in Heaven, when Moody developed the pschomantrium room.

Most Humans were satisfied with involving a third party for this purpose. Humans still often got distracted by other things and many didn't have the time or inclination to study for the many years it took to truly master the art of direct communication with the dead.

Angela got a kick at how similar Hattie's daughter's job on Earth was to her job in Heaven.

Angela knew the value of communication on all levels, and between all species. She had often been sadden by her own observations of what had happened to many of the animals, fish and bird species on Earth, over the millions of years since God had created the universe and Earth, in particular. Being an Angel, Angela was privileged with the knowledge of Earth's history.

But now, thanks to one of her conversations with Sonya, she had learned that Human's were now able to communicate directly with animals. Sonya had told her about her education process, as Angela had asked how Sonya had learned to communicate with her. Sonya, also told her that before she could even get to this plane of communication, her class had to study animal languages and learn to communicate with the mammals still on Earth. Sonya had told Angela how interesting and how much fun it was to learn about animal life directly from a porpoise or dog or orangutan. Sonya couldn't believe how easy it actually was to understand the minimal needs and wants and thoughts of animals compared to the intricacies of Humans' needs and wants and thoughts.

Sonya did tell Angela, much to Sonya's surprise, that it was very similar to the way a mother communicates with a new born baby, at least until the baby can talk and communicate for itself. All a Human really needed was empathy, compassion and most of all, love. Sight and sound helped in the Human world, but almost any of the senses could make communication between Humans and the animal world, possible, if Humans would only open themselves up to it.

Sonya told Angela how amazed she was that Humans, in the past, had only used such a tiny percentage of their brain.

Angela could definitely relate to Sonya's amazement. It was similar to the way Angela had felt once she arrived in Heaven.

Part of Angela wished that she had been as smart as Sonya was, while Angela lived on Earth. But, in the scheme of things, Angela knew that it really didn't matter when one learned of these things, as long as every one did, some day, even if it wasn't until they arrived in Heaven.

We all have our own time line for learning every thing.

Angela figured out that that was what made God's Plan so awesome and miraculous.

We'd all get there eventually.

"Praise the Lord," Angela sang on high.

37

Kaitlynn

1951

Kaitlynn had finished writing her memoirs two years ago. Her book 'A Woman on Her Own', had recently been published and was selling very well. This book was considered required reading for any woman who dreamed of or was living as a single female, or is involved with any facet of Women's Rights.

Kaitlynn's reputation, strength, determination, character and success were held up by the suffragettes as a real American woman role model to aspire to. Her illness, on top of all he successes, made her book very poignant. She received thousands of letters from women all over the country, who could relate to Kaitlynn's life and life's struggles. Kaitlynn shared many of the letters that she had received from the women who had read her book, in her newspaper column 'Women's Issues.' Many hidden issues that women have been trying to cope with for years, were brought to the fore front of the public's consciousness through Kaitlynn's column.

In particular, was the issue of domestic violence. There was no recourse for women these days, who had been beaten, maimed, or murdered by their husbands. This dirty secret had been continually swept under the carpet, up until Kaitlynn began to make this problem more widely known.

Both the government and religious communities, believed that men could, and did, have total control over their wives. Because of the male dominated society and court systems and religious factions, women had no place to go to find help or safety. They had had to suffer alone and silently, unprotected through most of history.

Because of the atrocious stories that were being relayed to Kaitlynn through letters, Kaitlynn felt that a call to arms to make domestic violence another feminist cause. She became one of the first women to attempt to bring this issue of violence against women to the public table.

Along with this issue of domestic violence, came the issues of child abuse. The early thought of the day was that there was some kind of correlation between the two problems.

After Tanya, Kaitlynn's personal assistant, had her daughter, Colleen who had been born mildly retarded, Tanya told Kaitlynn about her childhood with a neglectful mother and an abusive father. Tanya had been a victim of incest and Colleen was the result of this horrible, insidious crime.

Kaitlynn's pain and concern over what had happened to Tanya, enraged her and gave her the motivation and energy to front these very important issues.

Tanya also got involved and became very active in these causes as she had an important story to share. She accompanied Kaitlynn to many rallies and speaking engagements and participated by telling the audience her story.

Kaitlynn often wondered why Tanya never aborted this child-product of incest and rape. Tanya explained that her mother didn't believe that her second husband, Tanya's dad, did this to her. Her mother would not support or condone an abortion. Tanya's parents considered themselves good Christian people and regarded an abortion as a severe sin that would condemn any woman who had one, to hell. Apparently, they considered an abortion a worse sin than the sin of incest or rape.

Most of society, at his point in time, believed that 'a man's home is his castle and he could do whatever the hell he wanted to do in his castle.' The courts, legal communities, and police stayed out of a man's castle. They collectively believed that what happened in a man's house was none of their business, and therefore, they didn't get involved. Society preferred to turn a blind eye to these grave issues.

As sick as Kaitlynn was with scleroderma , she put her medical needs and physical discomforts aside as best she could. Domestic violence and child abuse were too serious for her to ignore.

Kaitlynn used a great deal of her own money to publicize and form organizations, where like minded people could get together to figure out what they could legally do to try and prevent these issues from escalating any further. Kaitlynn even contacted Alantra's father, Paul Taylor, who had been elected to Congress and , for several years now, had been residing in Washington, D.C. Paul agreed whole heartedly to do what he could, after hearing some of the horrendous stories that Kaitlynn related to him. Paul and Kaitlynn, helped co-author some bills and arranged several congressional hearings where domestic violence and child abuse were finally, for the first time, brought into the midst of the male hierarchy of the United States Government. Unfortunately, not much would change, regarding the punishment of men for these crimes, in Kaitlynn's or Paul's life time.

Kaitlynn and Paul had remained good friends over the years. Occasionally, Kaitlynn would stop and wonder what her life would be like now if she and Paul had gotten married. Paul had asked Kaitlynn, many times to marry him over the last several years, but it just wasn't to be. Kaitlynn felt pangs of remorse now and then. She knew they would have been a pretty decent couple, but she also knew that she was far too independent and had very little room in her life to fit in a partner.

Kaitlynn's and Paul's daughter, Alantra, took a six month leave of absence from her religious order to help take care of Colleen and Kaitlynn. She also wanted to help Kaitlynn and Tanya with their work on these new causes.

Kaitlynn, Alantra and Tanya, all fell in love with Tanya's daughter Keanna. Keanna was a very sweet and loving child. Although, very slow compared to most normal children, she was learning to talk and walk and function as well as could be expected considering her handicaps. Keanna was totally doted on and wanted for nothing. She was deeply loved.

Kaitlynn was determined to do what ever she could to keep Tanya and Keanna as happy as possible. Both had had a terrible beginning in life and Kaitlynn hoped that she could help make up for some of their pain, by giving them a warm loving family and home. Alantra felt the same way. Many other daughters, put in to a similar situation might feel threatened or jealous, but Alantra knew her mother had plenty of love and kindness to share with whoever needed some.

Together, they made as solid of a family unit as any traditional family could hope for.

Kaitlynn, now 60 years old, had plenty of assistance, not only from Alantra and Tanya, but from dozens of women in the women's rights organizations. Her house was a constant hub-bub of activity. Kaitlynn dictated letters, her column and instructions to a team of typists who were kept constantly busy. Kaitlynn paid her assistants well, and many of the women were able to get themselves out of poverty or out of a terrible marriage, and have a decent life.

They were very loyal to Kaitlynn.

Kaitlynn was constantly amazed at how many women, just in her own small world, were or had been victims of abuse and she had never known. That's how pervasive, secret and insidious these abuse crimes are and probably had been throughout time.

Kaitlynn, being a realist, knew that at her age and with her disease, she would probably not see many changes for the better, regarding women's plights, in her life time. But, she had been assured by Tanya, Alantra and most of the younger women involved with the women issues of the day, that she knew, would carry on.

38

Hattie

2041

Hattie and Jared had just finished dinner and were settling on to their huge over stuffed sofa to watch the latest communiqué, video that they had just received from their sons, Jason and Justin.

Communication from outer space could be sent any where at any time. It worked much like the way E-mail had worked in the late 20th century. The visual E-mail could be stored indefinitely if the receiver was not on line or home at the moment it was sent.

Hattie and Jared had several days worth of visual letters to catch up on. They had been away at a retirement seminar held in Boston, Massachusetts. Now that they were retired and still in good health, they were trying to decide where they wanted to spend the rest of their healthy life at. They knew that should one of them become ill, they would have to go in to a senior center, but that could be years away. They also had to decide what they wanted to do with the rest of their lives. If they wanted, they could continue working at the biosphere as there was no longer a mandatory retirement age. But they did have the choice of either working or living leisurely or both. One's working life could go on well past ninety years if one's health was up to it. Jared and Hattie had saved a good deal over the years and were presently considering their future options. Financially, they didn't need or have to work any longer.

Hattie had also received a large inheritance from her parents estate. This was quite an unexpected wind fall. Hattie's parents had always lived moderately and had managed to save a substantial amount of money.

The first few of the visual communiqué's from the boys were funny, newsy and nothing too interesting. The last one, however, was a different story. As the visual continued, both Hattie and Jared were sitting on the edge of the sofa. Their eyes were wide open in awe and their mouths were agape with surprise.

Jason, their oldest son, was introducing his parents to an extraterrestrial he had met while on one of his travels to another galaxy. The ET appeared to be of female origin and vaguely resembled a Human. She had two large dark almond shaped eyes, no nose, a thin mouth, no hair, two arms and two legs. Her skin had a bluish hue to it. She was dressed in a one piece dark metallic blue tunic-type garment.

Hattie had often in the past, read about the many UFO sightings, and more recently, landings on Earth. She had read about the American Government meeting with several extraterrestrials over the past several years. But neither Jared or Hattie had ever actually seen one up close.

At the turn of the century, the government, after years of cover ups and intense public pressure, finally released previously classified documents dating back to the 1947 Roswell, New Mexico, UFO crash incident.

There had been many documented UFO sightings through out most of history, but the U.S. government had been silent and secretive of what they knew for fear that public knowledge of these incidents would scare the public and cause a major panic.

On the visual communiqué, Jason had just mentioned the ET's name.

"Quick rewind the tape. I didn't catch the name," said Hattie excitedly to her husband.

Jared hit Rewind, and then Play.

"Her name is Ciaira (CE-air-a). Ciaira White." Jason said.

Jared stopped the tape. He and Hattie looked and stared at each other, dumbfounded at what they think they just heard.

"Did Jason say Ciaira White?" whispered Hattie.

"I, I, uh, think so," stuttered Jared. Jared hit Play again and they listened and watched the rest of the tape.

Their son Jason, now 32 years old, had married an extraterrestrial.

Hattie and Jared both simultaneously collapsed on the sofa. They had thought that they had kept up with all the advances, events and happenings of both their sons, Jason and Justin, up in the space colonies where both sons have been since finishing space training school. However, they had been very much unaware of any contact with other worlds, let alone any 'people' on these other worlds.

Hattie had a sense of revulsion come over her at the thought of having something not human as a member of her family.

It hadn't been that long ago since blacks and whites and the rest of the minorities had finally gotten use to each other and were now living in relative peace together as true equals. Race relations had improved steadily since the turn of the century, mostly due to all the natural disasters that had occurred and had naturally brought all races together to help each other out of these disasters. Human nature reverted back to real goodness and kindness during disasters. When people were fighting for their lives against the elements and mother nature, there was no thought given to the outward appearances of each other. At that moment of calamity, they were all in it together.

Bigotry was thought to be a thing of the past.

"Or was it?" Hattie pondered, upset about the way she was feeling about Jason's wife.

Meanwhile, Jared had placed a call to the nearest spaceport to find out if there was a chance that he and his wife could get on the next available space shuttle going to their sons space colony. He was told that they would need to undergo a six month training session before they would be allowed to fly on the shuttle.

Although international air travel had improved and one could now fly around the world in eighty minutes, outer space travel for the common man was far from being an every day thing. One had to undergo extensive training and medical testing before just anyone was allowed to fly to a space colony, let alone man one. This was because of the very very different 'living conditions' required to exist in space. Not every one was physically able enough to handle it. Up to now, only highly trained and skilled space cadets and astronauts were flown regularly in and out of space.

After finding all this out, Jared ended the call and rejoined a haggard Hattie on the sofa. After a long discussion their future was decided. They would undergo the six month space training program, so that they could visit their sons.

In the mean time, both Hattie and Jared wrestled with the conflicting thoughts, similar to the racists thoughts of the past, regarding their son, Jason, and his extraterrestrial wife. What did it all mean? What would the ramifications be if they ended up being grandparents to an unearthly being? They had many sleepless nights as they prepared for their space training ordeal and their pending first visit to outer space.

While Jared and Hattie waited for their appointment at space camp to undergo the training necessary so that they could visit their sons, Hattie would often wake up in the middle of the night. She would pace through out her condo thinking about her son's choice of marrying an extraterrestrial. She almost rather that he had chosen a renegade for a mate. At least renegades were Human.

Renegades were groups of people who had chosen to remain out side the bubble dome controlled environment communities. Most of them had seceded from the mainstream society in general. The renegades believed in living off the land with their own rules and regulations and with their own kind. They felt that they had more freedom by doing so. For the most part, the renegade groups tended to model themselves after 20th century motor cycle groups. Motorized bikes were their transportation of choice, as they were easier to maintain and used less gasoline, which was a good thing since gasoline was a rare commodity these days. Some renegades had adapted the use of solar or a more natural fuel made from human and animal waste.

Renegades were a hardy though motley group of people, believing in organic farming and were mostly vegetarians. Although occasionally they got lucky while fishing. Many tried to manage fish farms, but the vast pollution of the oceans and most water reservoirs, had been so extensive throughout the years, that finding untainted water was quite a feat. The renegades lived almost a nomads life style, moving frequently, depending on weather changes and or natural disasters which constantly changed the landscape and living conditions.

Some renegade groups were off-shoots of old white militia supremacist organizations that peaked in the late 1990's. Others were left over religious cult members who refused to assimilate into every day society, due to their odd beliefs and practices. Some were members from left over street gangs or former prisoners who had been released without authorization.

Many earthquakes had damaged most buildings including prisons and the escapees would hide among these various renegade groups.

Often there were territorial skirmishes between the various groups of renegades, and the news of these fights found its way into the mainstream newscasts.

Many members in the renegade groups, had a difficult time with other races, modern technology, government, families, loyalty, religion etc., etc., and reacted strongly whenever one group bumped into another group. Some groups tried to fortify their territory in fort-like structures, but, again, usually a natural disaster ruined the area and the group would be forced to move over and over again. The natural disasters were so wide spread that no place was left unscathed. A group may find relative peace for a few years in one location and then, POW, they'd be knocked for a loop by a major storm or earthquake or flood and they would have to start over again. Not to mention the death tolls they suffered as a result of the disasters or the skirmishes.

It was the government's thought, that most of these groups would eventually die out of their own accord, and tended to stay out of the renegades business. Many did die, but life had a way of continuing, depending on the survival skills and strength of each individual group.

In a normal society, many of these people would have chosen to live as an out cast any ways. So the fact that large bands of people with like interests bonded together, was no surprise.

The United States' government had given up on trying to rein in these renegade factions after many violent confrontations in the past. The government decided after years of debates and battles to no avail, to concentrate on the majority of society who chose to conform and live in the bubble dome communities. Resources of money, food, medicine and other government programs were limited due to all the disasters. It was finally realized and accepted that the governments of the world could no longer accommodate every one.

Hattie realized that she had led a very sheltered life, both as a child and then as a married woman. Part of her admired the renegades and their spunk for non conforming. She did understand that not every one could live with any kind of restraints and the bubble dome environments definitely constrained.

Many facets of modern day life were much stranger than fiction. But humans were adaptable, and as long as a human had free will and could choose the easy way over the hard way and vice versa, there would always be alternative and conflicting life styles.

Hattie contacted her daughter, Sonya, and told her that her brother, Jason, had married an extraterrestrial. Sonya was thrilled by the news and couldn't wait to meet Ciaira.

Hattie was puzzled by her daughter's positive reaction to, what Hattie considered, bad news. Sonya told her mom that she had been communicating with several aliens through her mental telepathy, mental teletransport and out of body experiences for several years now. She hadn't told her parents because this information had only been privy to her peers and they had agreed to keep it quiet until actual physical contact was made.

Hattie was stunned by the reality of how little she knew about any of her children. She began to feel those old anxiety attacks that she had suffered from as a child and young adult. Part of her wished her old wish that she could go back in time and be a pioneer woman of the 19th or 20th century, when life was simpler and made more sense, at least , to her.

She prayed to God for guidance.

39

Heaven

Angela was instructed by God to help ease Hattie's fears and concerns for her children. God had told Angela that a very important world event was about to take place.

Angela wasn't quite sure what God expected her to do in this regard. Personally, she was happy to see that some Humans, particularly Jason and Sonya's acknowledgment, acceptance and excitement on finally meeting beings from other worlds. Angela supposed that since these were Hattie's children, that that was why it was important for her to be assisted with handling this momentous situation.

"After all," Angela thought, "It has been written that God has many mansions. What had Humans thought that meant after all this time?" She knew that Humans were quite smug in their thinking that they were 'IT'. With the vast amount of numerous sightings of UFOs throughout Earth's history, one would have thought more Humans would believe in life on other planets and in other galaxies. But again, Angela knew the difficulty and limitations most Humans have with dealing with anything beyond their own reality.

Up until this point of time, Angela had been unable to share one of her own life experiences on the Planet Hades, with any other Earthling. Where as, most of Angela's angel- friends and families, many who had also lived in other universes, communicated often about their various past life experiences.

Now Angela would be able to share some of this information with Sonya, now that Sonya was aware and open enough.

Angela and many other spirits often had a great chuckle when they heard Humans refer to Hades as this terrible mysterious negative place. It was a Human's superstition and their minimal use of their brain that led Humans to think of any reference to some place called Hades as a bad hellish place. Hades must have been made known by Hadian visitors to Earth over the past several hundreds of years. And due to the Human ignorance condition, they did not understand what they were seeing or hearing regarding the 'possibilities' of aliens and UFOs. Their fears permeated their so called logical minds, and they treated the information of Hades as a fairy tale, legendary or through ancient Greek mythology, as a terrible place people went to after death if they were bad.

When the now ancient Greek culture was thriving, a few over zealous spirits in Heaven thought that the civilization on Earth had reached its pinnacle regarding growth and technology, life style and society. These spirits so believed that Earth was ready, that they took it upon themselves to communicate with 'aliens' (a Human term) or beings from other planets and civilizations, and told them to meet the Human Beings on Earth.

God had been quite upset about this turn of events. He knew that many spirit-souls were anxious and restless to rise to a higher level. But God knew that these rebel-spirits still needed to learn more patience, and , not too mention , that the Humans were not evolved enough to deal with other beings yet. Everything would happen in due time, as only God knows when that time would be. He convened a major meeting of all the souls in Heaven and gave strict instructions to not interfere on Earth unless he instructed otherwise .

With that direct message from God, the Hadians returned back to their home, or planet, leaving much mystery and many unanswered questions on Earth. The gossip and stories started and continued up through present time on Earth. It was also at this time that many many spirits opted to return to Earth in new lives to help push the progress-issue forward. God had given the rebel-spirits this option, that if they wanted to 'move' things along they could be reborn and assist in that way. As a result of a bigger Earth population, things were changing and advancing much quicker, and was becoming more noticeable by the other planets.

Angela was excited with the anticipation and hope, that finally the different beings, in all of God's mansions, would begin to physically meet each other.

"Oh Happy Day!" Angela sang softly to herself. She knew that exciting times were ahead. The level of absolutely everything would go up several planes.

Angela was full of joy, that finally, Human Beings on Earth had had enough of self- interest, and were now more willing, open and able, to share their existence with, at least the possibility, of others.

"Oh, dear Earthlings! You are in for some wonderful and delightful times," said Angela knowingly.

Angela was lucky enough and wise enough to know that if Everyone gets bumped-up to a higher level of knowledge, so does she. And she could hardly wait to see more of Heaven.

40

Kaitlynn

1956

Kaitlynn had recently returned from Washington, D.C. It would end up being her last trip to the East Coast. She had been invited to a personal meeting with President Dwight D. Eisenhower. He had learned of her vast amount of important work regarding domestic violence and he wanted to meet this woman who had caused such a national stir and an increase awareness through her articles in magazines and most newspapers about this topic.

President Eisenhower assured Kaitlynn that he would do everything in his power, to sign into law any legislation regarding violence in the home, that worked its way through Congress and the Senate and made its way to his desk.

Kaitlynn thanked him and returned home to San Francisco. She was thrilled that she had been fortunate to fly both to and from Washington, D.C. The flight was pretty rough and bumpy and included twenty other passengers. But she knew that flying would only get safer and better. She was just grateful that she had been able to fly again. She hadn't been up in a plane since her dear departed friend, Amelia Earhart, had taken her and her daughter, Alantra, flying years ago.

Kaitlynn had been devastated when Amelia had disappeared, and probably crashed, somewhere in the Pacific Ocean back in 1937. Part of Kaitlynn wished that she had been the one to go out in a blaze of glory. She knew that Amelia would always be regarded as one of America's most lauded heroines.

Over the years, Kaitlynn had kept abreast of the growth of flying and flying machines. It was, and always had been her secret passion. She had been reading about the government's plan to travel into space and she knew that that too, would one day happen.

Kaitlynn was pretty much wheel-chair bound now. Her scleroderma had progressed in such a way that most of her muscles were very stiff and sore. Her skin was very tough, which greatly hindered and limited her physical mobility. But with the use of her wheel-chair and an assistant she was able to get around with less difficulty.

Kaitlynn had recently had to say good-bye to Tanya and Keanna. Tanya's only sister had just had a baby daughter, named Jennifer. Tanya had maintained a close relationship with her sister and felt the need to be around her now. She had left home several years ago.

Kaitlynn had bought Tanya a car in appreciation of all that Tanya had done for her over the past several years. Alantra helped pack up Tanya's car and she and Kaitlynn, with many hugs, kisses and tears, said farewell to their dear friend and her daughter, Keanna. Tanya would be driving cross country from California to the small town of Plymouth, New Hampshire, and a very different way of life.

Their friendship would remain intact as they planned to write and call regularly. Some how Kaitlynn knew that she would always be connected to Tanya, Keanna, and now, Jennifer.

Tanya would spend many hours baby sitting her niece Jennifer and telling her mesmerizing stories about this great old lady, Kaitlynn Smith, and all the great and wonderful things she had done in her life.

With Tanya and Keanna now gone, Alantra and Kaitlynn found more time to spend together. Because of Alantra being such a devoted nun and member of the Catholic Church, Kaitlynn began to feel a need to attend church. She wanted to totally understand her daughter's faith, love and devotion to her way of life.

Kaitlynn's life had been so different from that of her only child's. Kaitlynn had spent the bulk of her life helping others have a better life. She had been practically completely selfless in this regard. Now finding herself at age 65, ill, and no longer holding her full time job as a columnist for the San Francisco Examiner, as she had officially retired this year, she felt a tug to explore her spirituality.

It was time for Kaitlynn to sit quietly and take stock of her life. Over the years since she had fallen ill, she had often prayed to God for the strength to keep going with all her various worthwhile women's organizations, causes and with her writing. She realized that God had indeed been answering her prayers, as the women's movement was strong and on going. Many of the women leaders in the fore front, had worked with Kaitlynn, and now they and their daughters were carrying on the work Kaitlynn had started years ago.

Although Kaitlynn still served on many of the executive boards of these various organizations, she no longer actively spoke or wrote for them. She just couldn't do it any more.

Her visit to Washington, D.C., to see President Eisenhower, was her last official involvement. At the advice of her doctors, she had to stop all physical work.

Kaitlynn had become very wealthy over the years. Now it was time to enjoy the comforts that her money could now provide. But since complete idleness would never be accepted by her, she became some what involved in her church. She tried to attend mass regularly, and decided that she would pray daily for all people, and for an end of all the problems that plagued the world.

Praying was now her main function. It was something that she could do any where, any time, any place. It was something worthwhile that she could do no matter how sick she became.

Alantra marveled at her mother's newly developed devotion. Her mother truly believed in the power of prayer and told Alantra how prayer had seen her through the hard years that she had struggled with scleroderma. She now wanted to share her knowledge of the power of prayer by setting a good example. Alantra and Kaitlynn often prayed together, outside in their beautiful flower gardens that over looked the San Francisco Bay.

41

Hattie

2046

Hattie and Jared were now the renown grandparents of a bi-terracial grand daughter, named Chy-Chy (pronounced chE-chE) White.

This was the first known successful mating of two different planetary species. Once the media had learned of this birth, they had reported on the story unrelentingly.

Hattie and Jared were the focal point of hundreds of articles, news casts and talk shows. Hattie had never in her wildest dreams, thought that she would ever be in the spot light like she and the rest of her family had been in for the past couple of years. Part of her enjoyed all the attention. Hattie remembered her fascination with news casts and talk shows about world-wide events when she was little. Now she was the one on the television, involved in the story of the Century. Some news casters called it the most historically important event of all times.

It all started after she and Jared had completed the extensive six month training ordeal they had had to under take so that they could visit their oldest son, Jason, and meet his extraterrestrial wife, Ciaira.

Hattie and Jared had passed the physical and medical tests with flying colors. Thanks to the medical advances of the past fifty years, they were both in excellent health. They had proven to have the stamina and enough physical agility that was required for any one flying faster than the speed of light, that was needed to travel to the very distant space colonies.

Prior to Hattie's and Jared's trip, Hattie had informed Jason of their pending visit. Jason, having not seen or hugged his parents in years, was extremely excited. He told them that he would get in contact with his brother Justin, who worked on a different space station, and make all the arrangements so that they can all have a great reunion and visit together.

Even their daughter, Sonya, prepared for the trip, as she had also gone through the six month space training program with her parents. Once Sonya had learned of her parents intention of visiting Jason and Justin, she prepared herself to go. She hadn't seen her brothers in years and wasn't going to let this opportunity pass her by. Sonya was also very curious to meet her new sister-in-law.

This visit would be the White family's first complete family reunion in about fifteen years.

Sonya was excited beyond words.

Hattie was nervous as hell.

Jared was full of trepidation.

The trip itself, via hypersonic transport, took a couple of months. The space colony was several millions of miles from Earth. For most of the trip, the passengers were put in coma-like states of deep deep sleep. The only way the human body could handle the immense physical stress that such a lengthy space trip, and the incredible rate of speed of the space ship placed on the physical body was by making the body completely relaxed. Their bodies would be fed and drained via IV's and catheters. Space travel was quite an ordeal even for experienced astronauts.

The trip proceeded without a hitch.

Once the space ship arrived at the space colony, it docked at the receiving door.

Hattie, Jared and Sonya and about sixty other passengers, now space travelers, were awaken from their deep sleeps. They were then led into a rest area within the space station where they could take showers and refresh themselves with real food and beverages. A nap wasn't necessary as al the passengers were well rested and wouldn't have to deal with jet-lag. They were then checked out by several different doctors who checked all vital signs and then released to go on about what ever business had brought them so far out of their normal environment to the space colony.

Jason and Justin were anxiously awaiting for their long over due family reunion with their parents and big sister, Sonya.

After many hugs, kisses, tears and smiles, things quieted down and Hattie was able to finally ask her son Jason, "Where's your wife, son?"

"Ciaira's back at our living pod. She is a bit nervous, and we had been forewarned that there may be some reporters flying in with you. Ciaira's a little shy," Jason said with a big grin.

"You'll love her, mom," piped in Justin, who had already met and become good friends with Ciaira.

"I can't wait to meet her!" said Sonya breathlessly. "I have wanted to meet a real life ET for ages."

"The word ET is a bit primitive, Sonya," explained Jason. "They prefer to be called by their names individually, or as a 'Terri' when referred to as a group."

Hattie and Jared looked at each other with raised eye-brows, took a deep breath and followed their sons out of the spaceport and into the main lobby of the space colony.

The colony or space lab, looked very much like a biosphere on Earth, except, of course, that it was floating in deep space. The colony was continually traveling farther and farther out into space. But because of the vastness of space itself, the colony appeared to be almost standing still.

The White family soon arrived at Jason's space pod. It was small, yet big enough to accommodate six people comfortably. It was a very functional, modern living quarter.

It reminded Hattie of the inside of a Winnebago that she and her parents use to travel in during their vacations in the 1980's and 1990's when she was a little girl.

Sitting at a table in what appeared to be the kitchen area, was the extraterrestrial (or Terri).

"Mom, Dad," Jason started with a deep breath," I'd like you to meet my gorgeous wife, Ciaira."

Hattie and Jared paused, now that the moment had arrived that they had so diligently prepared for, they did not quite know what to do or say.

Hattie gave Ciaira a nervous small smile and extended her hand.

Ciaira stood up and bowed before Hattie and then bowed toward Jared.

"This is my big sister, Sonya," continued Jason with the introductions.

Sonya, taking her cue from Ciaira, bowed to Ciaira, and they both smiled at each other. Sonya knew at that moment that they would get along just fine.

Hattie and Jared then also bowed to Ciaira, following their daughter's lead.

Ciaira then gestured with a wide sweep of her bluish colored arm.

"Have a seat Mom and Dad," explained Jason. He went on, " Terri's do not verbally communicate."

"Then how do you talk to each other?" asked a confused Hattie.

"Mostly through mental telepathy and hand gestures, a kind of sign language."

"That must be very difficult," said Jared shaking his head in disbelief.

While Jason explained their differences, Ciaira and Sonya prepared refreshments. Sonya immediately began using her earthly mental skills that she had honed expertly over the years, and started communicating directly with Ciaira. Ciaira's big dark eyes widened with, what appeared to be, surprise and happiness as she found herself able to quickly decipher and tune in to her new sister-in-law.

After the refreshments were served, Jason went over to his wife and put his arm around her thin blue shoulders. "We have more good news," said Jason, as he gave his wife a gentle squeeze. "We're expecting your first grand child," he said proudly to his whole family.

Hattie almost passed out, while Jared started to hyperventilate.

Sonya clapped her hands with delight and exclaimed, "How wonderful! I'm so happy for both of you!" Sonya also repeated the same sentiments to Ciaira through mental telepathy.

Ciaira, with a deep sincere nod of her head and a hand over her chest area, gratefully thanked Sonya for her good wishes.

Hattie and Jared were basically speechless. They honestly did not know what to say, let alone, how to say it.

Justin noticed that his parents were in a state of shock and quickly offered to take them on a tour of the colony so that they could catch their breath and gain some composure, get their bearings. He understood that this news was a lot to take in all at once, and especially in such a foreign environment.

Jason decided to go with his brother and his parents. He could tell that his sister and his wife would be fine alone together.

While Hattie, Jared, Jason and Justin toured the space colony, Jason told his parents how Ciaira and he had met. He had been on a mission to a newly discovered planet called 'Crystalmel'. He and his space troop had been ordered by N.A.S.A. to travel there and try to make contact with the beings that were discovered living on the planet. They had spent several months there and had learned a lot about the Crystalmel culture. Jason told his parents that, although physically there were some differences, culturally they were very much like the Crystalites.

Jason told his parents that Ciaira was the daughter of one of the leaders on the planet, and through many meetings and negotiations between the Earthlings and Crystalites, it was decided to experiment with the mating possibilities. Both Jason and Ciaira gallantly volunteered their service to their countries to be the first participants in the cross-culture experiment. Both had been highly honored and generously rewarded by their superiors for their willingness to join together. They would be given anything they needed and wanted so that the two of them could concentrate on each other without distractions.

Hattie asked her son when the baby was due. She also mentioned that she hadn't been able to tell that Ciaira was pregnant, as Ciaira was so thin.

Jason explained how the Crystalites only birthed strictly in-vitro. There was no actual sex act like what two humans experience. The male's sperm and the female's egg, were simply extracted and then technically incubated until the fetus was mature enough to be 'let out of the lab', so to speak.

Hattie thought that this was very cold hearted, yet she felt some relief at the sterility of it all. She had a very hard time picturing her son being intimate with such a different creature.

Hattie and Jared had to be given some leeway for their ignorance. After all, they were about to become the first Human grand parents of a bi-terracial child on Earth and maybe in the whole universe. (Which is a lot bigger than anyone can imagine.)

"Mom, I'm doing this for God and my country," said Jason proudly. "And besides, I have grown to truly love Ciaira. She's wonderful!"

All Hattie and Jared could do under these circumstances, which they had absolutely no control over, was accept their son's choice and learn to live with whatever comes of this union.

"When is the baby due?" asked Hattie, trying to sound enthusiastic.

"In about a week," said Jason.

"Oh dear," said Hattie, looking for a place to sit down before she swooned again. After a long pause, she told Jason, "Well, I guess we'll be here for the birth." They had planned on a two month visit any ways.

The week went by very fast. In that week, Hattie and Jared got to know and better understand Ciaira and her different ways. Ciaira had shown nothing but respect, courtesy and kindness to Jason's family. Hattie began to understand her son's love for Ciaira. She was very nice.

The birth-day had arrived. The baby was a girl. Ciaira and Jason named her Chy-Chy. It was a family name on Ciaira's mother's side.

Ciaira immediately offered her baby to Hattie to hold first. Hattie, a bit hesitant, took a deep breath and held out her arms. She was trying to prepare herself for what she might see. She had had several night mares this past week, waking up with the fear that the baby may look like some kind of monster or freak.

Hattie nodded to Ciaira, as she took Chy-Chy in to her arms. Slowly she carefully checked out her first (and only) grand child.

Although the baby's skin had a blue tint, and had larger than average Earth-size dark black eyes, the baby appeared very human. The nose was a bit small, which wasn't surprising considering that Chy-Chy's mother had no nose, and Jason's was fairly prominent. Her mouth was thin lipped and looked human. Hattie continued her inspection. She opened the pink metallic quilted blanket and saw that Chy-Chy had two arms, two legs and a pin-hole sized belly button. Hattie turned the baby over and noticed that she had a human looking bottom and a female's genitalia. Hattie let out a sigh of relief. So far so good. Then Hattie went to hold the baby's hands and noticed that there were only three fingers on each hand. Two were regular fingers with a thumb-like third one. Her feet were club-like with four very very tiny stubby toes on each foot. The digit numbers and the baby's blue skin color were the only apparent major differences between a Human baby and a Terri baby.

Hattie continued looking at Chy-Chy and thought to herself, "I can live with this." She began to smile and coo to Chy-Chy as two small tears fell from her happy relieved eyes.

"She's beautiful," Hattie said directly to Ciaira.

Ciaira smiled and bowed deeply at her mother-in-law. The relief and acceptance was apparent and obvious to both of them. They had both passed the test.

Hattie fell in love with both Ciaira and Chy-Chy there and then.

Jared, seeing his wife's acceptance, shrugged his shoulders and took the baby into his arms.

Sonya showed her delight by hugging Ciaira and Jason close to her.

They were now, and again, one bigger happier family. And soon to be the most famous family in the history of the world.

42

Heaven

Angela was so proud of the way Hattie had accepted her bi-terracial grand child. Angela knew that Hattie and her family had been chosen on purpose by God for this first interplanetary relationship. It was the beginning of a wonderful 'marriage', so to speak, between God's 'mansions'.

Angela turned her attention to her other concern, Kaitlynn. She knew that Kaitlynn had been living with a very difficult disease, but she was full of admiration for all the leadership and compassion that Kaitlynn had given to others over her long life. Kaitlynn had shown much dignity and grace in the way she was handling the trying test of scleroderma.

Angela felt pleased, and great relief, that her mistake of so long ago had turned out to be two wonderful success stories.

But then again, so were most of the lives of Humans on Earth. Humans weren't always able to see the good of their lives. But Heavenly beings knew that all beings were worthwhile.

Even in a Human's darkest hours, when everything appears so hopeless, there is great beauty in the observation from Above, of each soul's vulnerability. That is the moment when a Human soul is most open to accept and receive God into their heart and life. This could be done by the Human turning to God, or by letting down their guard and reaching out for help from family, friends or professional therapists. Many

Humans think that it is better to be strong and self-sufficient and handle one's own problems. However, Angela wished that she could explain that, although it is of some value for one to have that inner strength, the act of reaching out to a fellow human being is more important and takes far more courage and guts to do. Many times a Human's stubbornness, pride or refusal to accept help or charity or suggestions is a result of that Human's fear. Fear is negative across the board. A Human who doesn't reach out is telling everyone around him that he does not trust them. This has always been a very difficult, but very important lesson needed to be learned.

There have always been many Humans who constantly fight the 'God-thing' their whole life. But Angela knew that if a Human truly appreciated the 'free will' gift that God has given to all spirits, even the toughest die-hard atheist would be thanking God for the ability to choose or reject Him.

Due to the increase of knowledge and wisdom that spirits receive once they arrive in Heaven, Angela knew that God thought well of atheists. The atheists were not living in fear. An atheist had to contemplate the possibility of a god in order to accept or reject the notion. In fact, an atheist probably thought about God more often than many of the so called Christians on Earth. The biggest detriment to a Human's soul is fear not non-belief.

Angela knew that God disliked the way the so called 'men of god' preached fear into the souls of their earthly followers. Who did these guys think they were? The Human concept of religion was man's conception, not God's.

The preachers, priests, elders, reverends, etc., etc., who used fear to control the people into following their words, and used fear to gain wealth, and used fear to create more bigotry and racism in their followers, were in for a major shock and surprise after death when they finally face their Judgment Day.

After a person dies and before he can enter Heaven's Pearly Gates, one must go through a review of one's complete life and re-feel one's past sins and triumphs. One will feel both sides of every situation. Every wrong one did upon another, one will feel how the other person felt.

Many of Earth's religious leaders are ignorant to how much they are really hurting their fellow humans. Their motives may be good, but their techniques are often terribly destructive. There is always a right way or a wrong way to handle every situation, no matter how minor one might consider a situation to be.

God's will is that of Love; for every one, by every one. No ands, ifs, or buts.

Knowing all this was why Angela was so pleased with Hattie's and Kaitlynn's lives. Both of them were over coming their fears and becoming very loving human beings.

(Angela apologizes to the readers for sometimes sounding too 'preachy', but she often gets so upset at how hard, painful and fearful, Humans tend to make their lives. And it's so unnecessary. But then again, who would you rather have preach at you? A human man of the cloth or an Angel who's already earned her wings?)

God loves everybody!!!!!

43

Kaitlynn

1961

The past five years were fairly uneventful as far as Kaitlynn's personal life went. Although Kaitlynn was still quite sick, she continued her daily praying. She was also catching up on all the reading that she had been putting off for years because of her past busy life.

She had bought dozens of books over the years, but hadn't been able to read them until now. She also insisted that her personal attendant take her to the movies once a week. Being in a wheel chair actually made things easier for Kaitlynn to get around town.

Up until now, Kaitlynn had had little interest in television, movies or any other kind of show business. But now she was enjoying all kinds of movies, especially the animated movies from Walt Disney, like Snow White and Sleeping Beauty. It almost seemed like Kaitlynn was regressing a bit.

She had recently bought herself her first television set. She paid particular attention to as many news broadcasts as she could. It was important to Kaitlynn to keep up on current events. She missed her job at the newspaper for just this reason. She had always liked being on the cutting edge when it came to knowing what was going on in the world around her.

It was on her new television where Kaitlynn watched in awe and excitement, Alan Shepard, America's first astronaut, blast off into space in one of N.A.S.A.'s (National Aeronautics and Space Administration which was founded in 1958,) first successful manned rocket launches.

She wished that she could be in the rocket with Mr. Shepard. She tried to imagine the speed and thrill that Alan Shepard must have been feeling at the moment of blast off. It never even dawned on her that he might be scared silly. Fear was not a word in Kaitlynn's vocabulary.

She marveled at how she had always known that man would fly and some day fly into space. She imagined the beauty of flying through the star lit sky. Since she was a little girl, she had dreamed of being up there with the moon and the stars and all that space!

Sometimes she wondered why she had always been so interested in flying. She remembered the way her now deceased parents, John and Mary Smith, had ridiculed her when she would babble on and on about wanting to fly. But they hadn't been able to deter her interest and foreknowledge of flying. Sometimes she really thought that she had been born much too early. She would have rather lived in the future when flying was an every day thing and available to everyone.

In between praying, reading, watching television and going to the movies, Kaitlynn found herself reminiscing a lot about her life. She had done a great deal of traveling, met hundreds of interesting people and accomplished quite a bit in the past seventy years.

Her only regret was that she had never experienced being madly in love. Not even with Alantra's dad, Paul. She realized that she had never had the time for love and romance. She had experienced passion. Passion for women's rights and for flying. But she knew that that was a very different kind of passion that one could feel for a man. She was passionately in love with her daughter, Alantra, but that was a mother's love. That was nothing like what she imagined or pictured a love between a man and a woman could be like. Where she had been reading and watching love stories in novels and at the movies, she would feel a deep sadness at what she had missed out on.

Kaitlynn knew that she was much too old to ever expect such an experience to happen to her now.

She wondered why she had been so single minded all these years. It wasn't like she had never had the opportunity to meet the right man. She had met dozens of handsome successful men over the years in the course of her job at the newspaper and through all her travels.

She supposed though, that she had been more exposed to the negative side of men through the years. With all the time she had spent working and fighting for women's rights, she had seen first hand that the world was a man's world. She also saw first hand how disdainful most men considered assertive, strong and single women. She also heard hundreds of horror stories of abused women who had suffered at the hands of the men in their lives.

Kaitlynn had been fortunate to not have experienced any personal physical abuse from a man, unless of course she considered the sexual harassment she often got at work, or the numerous times she had been spit at, called names and prejudged by the many men during a woman's protest, march or strike.

She didn't think that counted, as there had also been many women who put down her views and work in very rude ways. She surmised that she had pretty much been called every bad name in the book by both sexes.

Her boss at the Examiner had often called her a 'real tough broad.'

She chuckled at that memory. She guessed that she had been one 'heluva tough broad'.

Kaitlynn had also been very impressed with the United States new president . A young Irish catholic man from Massachusetts, her home state. His name was John F. Kennedy. She liked his message and the many wonderful speeches he gave. She especially liked the fact that he was so young. In fact, John F. Kennedy was the youngest president ever elected in America, since America had presidents. Kaitlynn thought that only young men could truly maintain the stamina it took to run a country. She felt that men her age would better serve as mentors and confidantes and stay out of the lime light.

Kaitlynn found that in spite of the age difference, she agreed with most of Kennedy's points of view. She hoped that he would be able to fix many of the problems facing America today, especially regarding all the civil rights issues that were coming to a head.

Kaitlynn also liked watching the speeches of a young black man, Martin Luther King, who was also working for civil rights for his people.

She couldn't help but notice that more and more people were getting involved with the problems of the world and speaking out against injustice and demanding changes. She thought that this was a good turn of events. It made her recall all of her battles in the past. She wished that she had the energy to get back out there and work with Kennedy and King and help their causes.

But Kaitlynn thanked God for allowing her to keep living in spite of her illness. She had learned a lot about scleroderma over the years. As rare as this disease was, she felt pretty lucky compared to many of the others who had been stricken with the disease. Most died very quickly after scleroderma's on set. Her life had been some what spared. She had been given more time than what scleroderma usually allowed. She knew her praying had a lot to do with that.

Her daughter played a big part with extending Kaitlynn's life also. Alantra had helped weaned Kaitlynn off the codeine a few years ago, and through a healthy diet, aspirins and lots of prayers, Kaitlynn was hanging in there. So what if she had to wear diapers and eat baby food. She was still alive and she still had her clever, alert, clear mind. Her hearing was not so good, but her eye sight, with the help of glasses, was okay. What more could a person ask for?

Kaitlynn was thankful for what she knew was extra time on Earth, as she was able to witness with positive hope, all that was happening in the world today.

44

Hattie

2051

Hattie and Jared's only grand child, Chy-Chy, was now seven years old. Not only was Chy-Chy bi-terracial, she was also bilingual. She had learned to speak English and to communicate in her mother, Ciaira's, language.

Hattie enjoyed the regular visual communiqués they received from her son, Jason, and her daughter-in-law, Ciaira. Chy-Chy tended to hog the camera as she had quite a personality. Let's face it, she was a ham. She loved to dance and sing and even surprised her grandparents by levitating her dad up off the chair that he was sitting on. Chy-Chy also knew how to tele-transport items from one place to another.

Hattie had been unaware, up until now, that Ciaira and Chy-Chy had such skills, as neither she or Jason had ever mentioned these things before.

Jason, Ciaira and Chy-Chy were often on the news via the space colony. Because of all the media attention, the whole White family had become quite famous.

The fame had actually benefited Sonya and her metaphysical practice. She was constantly inundated with requests from new clients wanting to learn how to communicate with the 'Terri's'. Many of the requests came from government officials and military personnel.

Apparently, American's had opened their hearts and minds with acceptance of the extraterrestrials.

Many people sought the White family out to ask permission to meet Ciaira and Chy- Chy. However, that possibility was beyond Hattie's and Jared's control. The United States government handled all visitation and interview requests.

Chy-Chy was especially looked at as such an oddity and main attraction. Everyone wanted a piece of her. As it was, Chy-Chy was involved in many medical studies. Scientists and Doctors rushed to Jason's space colony as soon as Chy-Chy's existence became known. The whole scientific and medical communities, were anxious to test Chy-Chy's IQ and every other nook and cranny.

Feeling much love for Chy-Chy, and also now for Ciaira, Hattie couldn't help but worry about the ordeal that they both were being forced in to. With the media, scientific, medical and political frenzy surrounding Chy-Chy and her mom and dad, Hattie was concerned for their safety and well being.

Hattie did understand that both Jason and Ciaira had volunteered for this mating experiment, but she wondered if they had really thought of all the ramifications for their bi-terracial child that would incur.

Hattie also wondered what Ciaira's parents were like. Jason had told his parents that 'Terri' parents have very little to do with their children once they become full grown. On Crystalmel, Ciaira's planet and home, all adult 'Terri's' had very important technical functions, or jobs, and this took priority over family ties.

The whole planet sounded very cold-hearted to Hattie. As excited and amazed as she was at where her life and her family's life had taken them on Earth, she couldn't imagine life on another planet, let alone on Crystalmel.

Jason tried to explain how much further advanced technology-wise Crystalmel was compared to Earth. The Crystalites, or 'Terri's' had been visiting Earth (and who knows where else) for years. They had total control of their own atmosphere and weather. Their machines exceeded the intelligence of Humans on Earth. They could levitate, tele-transport and make themselves invisible at will. Their mental capabilities involved mental telepathy, reading minds, out of body travel and the ability to communicate with many different realms of spirits. They basically lived a life of immortality, meaning that they did not relate to death as a finality like most Humans did. This immortality belief came as a result of their being able to move freely between the different levels of spiritual realms.

Jason told his parents that Earth's clones were probably closer to being a 'Terri' than a Human was. The clones that Humans had developed, could technically last forever with only few, if any, maintenance tune ups required now and then. Although clones experience no feelings, no emotions and no health problems, they are programmed with high intelligence. With that level of intelligence most clones could figure out, with logic, how to handle most human- type problems. Whether the clones could teach Humans how to relate more Humanly and lovingly toward each other remains to be seen. The clones were definitely more courteous and civil than a lot of Humans, and Humans could learn that from the clones. Although, with logic, the clones could solve most problems, they had no idea about God and Heaven, other than text-book type references.

Hattie wondered if that meant that once Humans died out and all the other beings that may be out there, went to other spiritual levels, would the universe continue infinitely, to function under the mechanical clones control?

This thought was heavier and scarier than any Hattie had ever pondered before. Although she was more open to what once were unbelievable things to her, like her being able to relate to Kaitlynn, who was dead, and to her daughter-in-law and grand daughter, who were ET's, there were limits to Hattie's mental comprehension capabilities.

She figured that her daughter, Sonya, could probably deal with such thoughts better and easier than herself. After all, she had witnessed Sonya's channeling skills and her mental telepathy skills first hand. Hattie was filled with admiration at how quickly Sonya had been able to tune into and communicate with Ciaira. Sonya also, as if she didn't have enough to do, was now involved with teaching many government officials the art of mental telepathy and the communication skills needed to converse with extraterrestrials.

As Hattie thought back on her long seventy years on Earth, she had never ever imagined that life, and her life in particular, would have changed, or been capable of such changes as to keep up with all the rapid changes that had happened on Earth during her life time. It truly was mind boggling. Yet Hattie had to marvel at the adaptability of herself and her fellow Human beings.

If Hattie wasn't living her life, she would never believe it. She knew that if she had had a glimpse of her future life when she was a little girl, she would have probably opted not to live it. It would have scared the crap out of her. But then she realized that she wouldn't have met and fallen in love with Jared, who was a wonderful husband and friend. She wouldn't have had her three outstanding, wonderful now famous children. And she wouldn't have had the privilege of being Chy-Chy's grandmother.

Hattie recognized, now, that her life was a privilege (as is all life.)

Of all the people she had met and known throughout her entire life, she felt most grateful to her daughter Sonya. Sonya truly opened her eyes and mind. And Hattie was grateful to Kaitlynn, who opened her mind even more. With an open mind, Hattie realized, anyone could accomplish anything. An open mind was a plus. More knowledge was a plus. Learning was a real exciting trip.

Hattie's life was proof of how wonderful it was to be alive. Her children were proof. Jared was proof. What more proof did one need?

Suddenly, Hattie recalled her last communication with Kaitlynn. It had been several years now, since they had last communed. Kaitlynn had told Hattie how important prayer was.

How prayer had kept Kaitlynn alive longer even though she had a horrible disease. Hattie had listened to Kaitlynn, but didn't pay all that much attention to the prayer part of their last conversation. Hattie had always been 'too busy" with adjusting constantly to the many complicated changes that had been bombarding her most of her life, her family's life and life in the world in general.

Hattie had been some what religious when she was a young lady, but she remembered that most of her praying had to do with finding herself a husband. Her prayers never went beyond what she needed or wanted. She did remember thanking God for Jared, but then her 'religion' seemed to fade away. She hadn't needed the crutch that religion had provided her since she was young, miserable and depressed.

As she thought about how wonderful her life had been over all, she finally understood the type of praying that Kaitlynn must have been trying to get her to understand. Prayer for Mankind.

Hattie decided that it was finally time to learn how to pray the right way.

45

Heaven

Heaven had been on full throttle for quite some time. It seemed that Humans were finally learning and appreciating the power of prayer. Prayers were coming in so fast and furious that all the angels and spirits were on over-drive, doing their best to answer as many prayers as they could.

Angela's reunion department was particularly busy as more and more 'third-party' requests were being made to make contact with Earth-departed loved ones from their family and friends still alive and residing on Earth.

Many of Angela's underlings bombarded her with questions asking 'What was going on?"

Angela explained to them that one of her special wards had recently perfected the art of channeling and had recently published a 'How-To' instruction manual that could teach every day individuals how to self-channel.

Angela was thrilled that Hattie's daughter Sonya had been able to literally cross the spirit realm and was now sharing her skill and knowledge. Knowledge and intelligence are meant to be shared.

For years on Earth it seemed that only a few chosen individuals, who had learned to communicate with spirits, were up until now, coveting their knowledge and techniques of communicating with spirits. These particular Humans used this 'gift' as a means to gain wealth and power. The primitive ones were called psychics, who didn't take their god-given gift that one step forward, by learning how they were able to predict things. They just used the 'gift' to get rich and famous.

That was not God's intention for bestowing such a gift.

It took Hattie's daughter Sonya's gift to finally break that barrier. And her book did just that. Sonya's book had sold like hot cakes. And her books were the main reason for the sudden flurry of activity in Angela's department.

One would think that all angels would know everything about everything at the same time. But each angel had its own duties, its own group of Humans to watch over and needed to concentrate on their own responsibilities and wards. So unless something major happened, like what was going on now in Heaven and Earth, angels worked more on their own than as a group.

But now since more and more Humans were getting their act together the angels had to unite and get their act together. Not only were things apparently speeding up on Earth, they were speeding up in Heaven also.

Angela knew that it would eventually slow down some after Humans became more adept at handling their prayers and contacts in a more rational and routine fashion and became more comfortable with this knew use of their brains, intelligence and knowledge. Angela hoped that it wasn't just a new fad that Humans were playing with. She worried that this increase of praying would just run its course and then Humans would get on with their daily lives. Their concentration would then be able to be directed to dealing with the reality and acceptance of the extraterrestrials.

Angela knew that this was only the beginning as far as Humans interacting with the ET's on Crystalmel. There were more to come.

No one on Earth or in Heaven, except God of course, knew how long all of this interplanetary interaction would take.

However, Angela did know that as Humans grew, learned and accepted the different Beings, their existence on Earth will have risen several levels. Even Angela, who had been in Heaven for quite some time, still had much to learn. She often pondered at the enormous, practically infinite amount of knowledge to learn that was still ahead of her. She was often flabbergasted at how much she already did know. (Definitely more than Humans) With that knowledge, it became a little bit easier to comprehend how big the entire universe may be.

Angela would picture herself growing larger and larger as she learned more and more. (Not having a physical body, per se, it was a figurative picture.)

So far, knowledge appeared to have no foreseeable end in sight which may mean that Angela would get much much bigger. And then, she thought, ' if I get as big as the universe and all the other spirits get as big as the universe, and all the Beings on Earth, Crystalmel and all the other planets get as big as the universe, well, that's a pretty darn big space!"

This thought made Angela try to picture how big God must be. She could not comprehend this conception. Even though she was an angel, it was more than her angel-mind could deal with at the spiritual level where she was at.

"Phew," Angela said, "No wonder Humans give up sometimes."

Trying to master and comprehend something that, at a particular moment appears incomprehensible, can really really tire one out, not to mention discourage a person, spirit or Human.

Angela really understood why Humans spent so much time doing so many mundane boring things. She, an angel, was hardly equipped to handle the magnitude of this kind of thought and thinking process, and she was quite a ways ahead of all the Humans and other beings in the universe.

No wonder life often feels endless and hopeless to Humans.

Life is better lived one step at a time, one lesson at a time, one day at a time, one week at a time, one month at a time, one year at a time, one world at a time and one spiritual level at a time.

Angela knew that one reason Human technology seemed to advance and improve so quickly was the Human need to improve the act of living every day easier so that one could concentrate on learning. Learning didn't necessary mean that every one had to memorize or actually experience every little detail of History or that every major life lesson learned throughout time had to be comprehended. Awareness of life lessons was often enough for someone to understand and learn something. With awareness one intuitively could understand the good and bad of that particular situation. And that awareness was often enough to prevent one from repeating or making the same mistake as someone had before them. . An aware Being could decipher its basic needs and its lessons needed to learn at each level. This awareness is not always as obvious as black or white. But, if and when a Being takes the time to think about and reflect on a situation, event, or crisis, past or present, one will more often than not, learn what one needs to learn at that time and place. (Or what should have been learned from that happening.)

Angela knew that many things were easier said than done. Sometimes it took several repeats of the same or similar mistake before a Being 'got it right.' But evolution was such, that each generation has some foreknowledge, whether they are aware of it or not, of life prior to their existence level now. (Have you ever surprised yourself with just knowing something is so, and you have no idea how you knew? That is foreknowledge.)

Beings, very often learn big lessons by just being aware of all the Being's lives around them. (some people think that one can only know this kind of stuff if you study psychology, although that study topic can be very helpful, but who needs all those 'labels'). This is where love, compassion, empathy and good deeds prove to be such important Human traits to have and practice. Whenever a Being shares with another Being, their lives, their pain, their problems, their loves, their hobbies, their life lessons, they both, or the group as in support groups, learn from the experience of sharing. In other words, it is not necessary to learn or re- learn first hand, every little thing. We can learn from simply sharing with each other.

Angela knew the problems that can arise sometimes from the misconception that, especially as a Human, one might feel overwhelmed at life and all the problems that they know comes from just living. This is the awareness and foreknowledge that most Beings are born with. Although it seems more of the foreknowledge appears some what negative, most foreknowledge is actually positive. It all depends on one's outlook on life. Some Beings seemed blessed with having a more positive attitude, but one's attitude can always be changed or improved. So much does depend on what kind of a situation a Being is born into. But all Humans are born into the situations they need to be born in, in order to learn the particular lessons that God has deemed necessary for each very loved Being to learn or to teach to others. That's where the sharing becomes such an important Human trait.

Unfortunately, many Beings opt to cop out either through committing suicide or through the use of drugs, alcohol, promiscuous sexual activity, bad habits, some mental illness, religion and other bad choices of extreme life style behavior. Many Beings choose to defy life by pushing themselves to the edge through extreme physical limits of dangerous sports.

Angela also knew that there are many levels of life on Earth itself. Humans, in physical form, are not all on the same level of spiritual growth. This is also a difficult concept to understand and accept. Although Humans have tried to claim through political documents, that all men are created equal, how can this be? It's a nice idea , but if it was true wouldn't all Humans get along? Angela Knew that in God's eye, everyone was loved equally, but everyone had many many different purposes to serve on Earth. If everyone was the same there would be no problems of any kind on Earth. It would in fact, be more like Heaven, but even here there are still many levels. It was Angela's understanding, that yes, eventually All would be One with God and then maybe, everyone would be truly equal. But again, only God knows.

Angela knew that mankind's intention with the 'all men are created equal' statement that good intentions were the hope. But this 'tenet' was never practiced or completely believed by any one, and certainly not by anyone who had been put into power on Earth to make this 'tenet' work. It simply is not so. A person in power knows that in his mind, he is above the people supposedly following his lead. Whether his thought process is right or wrong, how can that be equality to all the people being ordered about? A person's age also determines where a person is in growth or rank. How can that be negated? Angela and many of her peers had wanted to sneak back to Earth and change the US Constitution to change the 'equal' statement, to read more like 'all people are to be treated with equal love and respect.' But that was not God's Plan. Man had to learn from his own mistakes.

Many of the loneliest Humans are more spiritually advanced . They are often alone because of the unavailability of another Human on the same level of awareness. The sad part about this advanced Human is their own lack of awareness or acceptance that this is why they are so alone. When one tries to relate and communicate at a depth that another cannot comprehend, its like talking to a wall. One doesn't get a response or certainly not the response the aware one hoped for. They are often treated as an outcast and picked on.

If a person appears to be living a life outside the conformity of the acceptable mainstream of society, that person is often looked at with contempt. Again, this is an element of fear by the mainstream group. When in reality the non-conformist is simply on a different level, either above or below the level of the group. But this is not for a Human to judge. Only God can judge.

It was hard being an angel sometimes. Especially when Angela and the other angels saw how terrible Humans could be to each other. They knew that they had to practice tolerance and not intervene on Earth unless directly instructed to by God. But it was difficult. If an angel could grit their teeth, that's what they'd be doing because of their frustration. Knowing what they know now being in Heaven they could so clearly see the mistakes happening over and over on Earth. And because angels truly love all beings, they only wanted to help. It was angel-nature.

At the end of the 20th century, many of these important group issues were coming to a head. Situations like racism, high divorce rates, increase of violent crimes, homophobia, militia and religious factions and all the copping out in general was getting out of hand.

Humans were separating from the 'norm' at a faster rate. Unfortunately many groups pulled away for very wrong reasons. However, there will be some very important lessons taught and learned as a result of the breaking up of society. On the other side of the coin, the need to pull away is very important. Until the majority are of similar spiritual growth levels, true harmony will be hard to come by.

There will be less human coupling because of diseases like AIDS. There will be fewer life long marriages, because humans have a greater need to be alone so that they can grow spiritually faster and develop important career choices that will do more to help mankind than hurt. Unless two humans are at the same level and can handle each other's individuality without becoming possessive and obsessive , marriage just isn't going to work any more.

A single life and intense career attention will require more energy and focus than ever before. The yearning for spiritual growth will surpass the old yearning to mate.

The Earth is becoming too polluted and its natural resources are being drained at a faster rate due to the enormous amount of population growth that had gone unchecked in the 20th century. There are more people on Earth now than the total amount of people that had lived in all the centuries before, combined. Fewer people will choose to have children. The selfish need to only have a child to carry on one's family name will fall to the wayside, as people come to recognize that we are all of the same family. Fewer spirits in Heaven will choose to reincarnate as more was learned and accomplished their last life time on Earth. There will be more group therapy and group conferences to satisfy the need for Human interaction. It will become very similar to the way life is for Angela and the rest of the angels in Heaven. When information needs to be shared, it will be shared and then back to the business at hand.

Angela knew that life would appear quite tough for awhile, but mostly because many Humans fought changes, again mostly out of fear of the unknown. But because of the increase of natural disasters that were already beginning to occur on Earth, the changes will happen out of necessity, and Humans will have to literally sink or swim, go with the flow and get with the program.

More Humans will begin to accept that life, although full of many pot holes and barriers, can and will be an exciting and worthwhile journey.

As medical and scientific technologies advance and improve life, Humans will become less focused on their physical appearance and with their material things. The quality of the physical life will take care of itself and more concentration and improvement of each person's spiritual growth will become the major concern. As it should be.

Angela decided that she too would concentrate more on her own praying. She had been a bit neglectful of late, but because she was aware of the glorious times ahead waiting for her and all of God's Beings, she knew that even the littlest of prayers would help. She also knew that things on Earth might appear to get worse before they got better, but she also knew that they will get better, sooner than we think.

Angela also chose to concentrate on her praying because everyone, angels included, needed all the help they could get. And prayers definitely helped.

46

Kaitlynn

1966

Kaitlynn's health was definitely going down hill. Scleroderma had it's strong grip on her, as did old age. She seemed to be losing her will to live. Ever since President John F. Kennedy had been assassinated on November 22, 1963 in Dallas, Texas, Kaitlynn had become very depressed. She had watched the whole ordeal over and over again as the events of that day and the funeral that followed were broadcast almost daily for weeks afterwards.

With Kennedy's untimely death, much of America's hopes and dreams for the United States' future seemed to have been killed and dashed along with his demise. Kaitlynn wasn't the only one to have been so affected by JFK's assassination. The assassination and the horror of that reality put a dark pall over the whole country and a large part of the rest of the world that looked to the USA for guidance and leadership. How could something like this happen in America?

JFK's murder, zapped Kaitlynn's faith in her fellow man, and with those hopeless feelings of loss, came a severe loss of her inner strength and desire to live on.

Alantra spent as much time as she could with her mother. She tried to nurse her mother's health as well as her spirit. Alantra had never seen her mother this depressed before, and in many ways, this depression was harder to witness than her illness had ever been.

It was a trying time for both Kaitlynn and Alantra. Alantra knew that her mom wasn't going to live forever, but to see her mother's last years become so dark and empty after having lived such a dynamic, busy and exciting life, was almost too much for Alantra to bear. It made Alantra question her own faith and religion. Although her life as a nun had been very rewarding and she had been quite content and happy with her choice, she now had conflicting troubling thoughts and doubts. If she was unable to help her own mother after she had helped so many others through the years, how could she consider her life as a nun successful? Even her prayers seemed useless.

Alantra could see that Kaitlynn was turning away from God and prayers when she really needed God and prayer the most.

Kaitlynn also lost all interest in reading and going to the movies. She stopped most of her correspondence with all of her friends. The only two people Kaitlynn seemed to still care enough about to write or call on the phone occasionally were her first personal assistant, Tanya, and Tanya's niece, Jennifer, who was now ten. There had been a very strong connection that had developed over the years between Kaitlynn and Jennifer. It was just one of those cosmic unexplainable connection things.

Because Alantra knew how much Kaitlynn loved Jennifer, she decided to contact Tanya in New Hampshire, and see if she could arrange a visit. Money wouldn't be a problem as Kaitlynn had more than enough to cover the costs. However, Alantra wanted this to be a surprise and had to come up with a skillful excuse to ask her mother for a few thousand dollars.

Having never asked her mother for money before since she was a nun and had taken a vow of poverty, she knew that Kaitlynn would probably be curious.

Well, Alantra was wrong about her mother being curious. Her mother didn't even blink an eye when Alantra asked for the money. She merely told Alantra to take what ever she wanted, take it all as she had no use for it any more.

Alantra was concerned about her mother's apathy regarding her money. It made Alantra all the more determined to get Tanya and Jennifer to California as soon as possible.

Alantra wired the money to Tanya in Plymouth, New Hampshire, and made and confirmed all the travel arrangements.

Tanya and Jennifer would fly out of Logan Airport in Boston, Massachusetts, and arrive in San Francisco, a month from now. Their visit would occur around May 11th, Kaitlynn's Birthday. Alantra would plan a huge birthday party. It would be Kaitlynn's 75th.

Kaitlynn pretty much stayed in her bedroom. She just did not have the strength, desire or gumption to get out of bed.

As concerned as Alantra was about that, it made her planning and preparing for Kaitlynn's surprise, visitors and party much easier. Alantra hired a caterer, a band and sent out over one hundred invitations. She phoned her father, Paul Taylor, now a retired congressman, and made sure that he would be at her mother's birthday party.

He would be there with bells on.

Neither of Alantra's parents ever married. That fact never really bothered her, although she often wondered why over the years. All three of them got along very well, better than most families, so there had never been any real sadness at never having been a normal family, whatever that was. Occasionally Alantra did wonder if her life would have been any different had Paul and Kaitlynn actually married. Alantra had been brought up around all kinds of single men and women her whole life. Her choosing to also live a single life was not that surprising. Well, the nun part was, as religion had not played a part in her up bringing as a young child at all. Kaitlynn and Alantra had talked about Alantra's so called 'calling' many times. All Alantra could tell her mother was that it was something she just had to do. Kaitlynn related it in the only way she could by her' calling', as a young woman, to go West. They both agreed that the 'callings', although different in direction, were kind of the same thing; that something unexplainable inside oneself that one cannot ignore.

The month passed by quickly.

Kaitlynn was still in her depressed funk, although part of her did wonder why Alantra seemed more excited than usual.

When Alantra was tending to Kaitlynn's daily needs of bathing and feeding, she chattered happily about nothing in general. This odd behavior of her daughter, did peak Kaitlynn's curiosity a little bit. Kaitlynn pretended to not show any interest but she kept a watchful curious eye on her daughter.

The morning of Kaitlynn's 75th birthday began as mundane as most of Kaitlynn's mornings had been over the past couple of years. However, Kaitlynn could detect a lot of commotion going on down stairs. She could hear lots of laughter and the sound of furniture being moved around as it scraped the wooden floors.

Alantra was spending more time with Kaitlynn on this particular morning's bathing routine. She took great time and care in washing and curling Kaitlynn's now totally white hair. Alantra had also dressed her mother in a lovely new silk dress and insisted that Kaitlynn was going out today. Kaitlynn argued half-heartedly with her daughter, but conceded and let Alantra help her into her wheel chair, which she hadn't been in for quite awhile.

Years ago Kaitlynn had a chair elevator, or stair-way lift, installed in her stair case, so that she could go up and down at will. As Kaitlynn slowly descended down her stair case, she saw Tanya and Jennifer at the foot of the stairs. Kaitlynn immediately broke into the biggest happiest smile. Her depression evaporated. A tearful joyful reunion with lots of hugs and kisses and exclamations of joyous surprise were exchanged.

Kaitlynn tenderly embraced Jennifer for the longest time. She gently took little Jennifer's face into her two stiff, hard wrinkled old sclero-derma hands, and with tears streaming down her face she said, " Oh my dear, dear, Jenny. I am so happy to finally meet you."

They had written for years and Kaitlynn had only, up until now, seen photographs of Jennifer.

Jennifer giggled with delight and told her Auntie Kate, as that's what she had always addressed Kaitlynn as in her letters," You are as beautiful as I always knew you'd be."

Alantra stood behind Tanya and watched her mother and Jennifer hug and exchange kisses. For one brief moment she thought that they looked and acted more like a "mother and daughter" than just good friends. The way Jennifer immediately helped Kaitlynn into her down stair wheel chair and assigned herself as Kaitlynn's keeper was a wonder to behold.

Jennifer pushed Kaitlynn into the main living room where Kaitlynn was then greeted by Paul and dozens of old friends she hadn't seen in years. Even her old boss from thenewspaper was there.

The party ensued and everyone had a grand time. Especially Kaitlynn.

This was exactly what the doctor had ordered, thought Alantra, pleased with herself.

As Kaitlynn greeted and exchanged words with all her guests, Jennifer waited on Kaitlynn, hand and foot. Jennifer could not do enough for her.

Finally Kaitlynn told Jennifer, 'You are going to make some one a wonderful mother some day."

Paul then came up to Kaitlynn after the cake, ice cream and champagne had been served, and sat down beside her. He lovingly took her hand and told her how wonderful she looked.

Jennifer discreetly left Kaitlynn's side and joined her Aunt Tanya and Alantra on the other side of the room.

Kaitlynn said to Paul, as she watched Jennifer go over to her aunts, "Isn't she wonderful?"

"She's lovely," said Paul. "I always told you that should have had more children."

"I know," said Kaitlynn with a sigh. "But it's a bit too late for that, don't you think?"

Paul chuckled and agreed as he thought about how much time had passed since their daughter Alantra had been born. "We should have gotten married, you know?" Paul said softly.

"You don't give up, do you?" said Kaitlynn with fondness in her voice.

"It's still not too late…" he said wistfully.

Kaitlynn took Paul's large hand and kissed it affectionately, and gently said, " Paul, what we had was better than a marriage. We're great friends. We respect each other and we have a wonderful daughter."

Paul nodded in agreement and added," We love each other, too."

"Yes," Kaitlynn said with a slight pause. "Yes we did, in the best possible way. you let me live my life and I let you live yours."

They smiled at each other and embraced.

In that brief moment, Kaitlynn finally realized that she had loved Paul deeply ever since they first met. She had been kidding herself all these years wondering when she would meet her soul-mate. He had been right under her nose the whole time.

"'We get too soon old and too late smart'," Kaitlynn quoted from something she had read, but she couldn't remember when.

At the moment Alantra came and interrupted her mom and dad. "Time for photos everybody!" Alantra ordered.

Flash bulbs started popping as Paul, Kaitlynn and Alantra posed, and then Kaitlynn and Jennifer posed.

These photographs showing great joy and happiness, would long be cherished as they documented the last years of Kaitlynn's life.

47

Hattie

2056

Hattie's youngest son, Justin, had died unexpectedly over a year ago. He and a group of space explorers had been on a mission to check out a newly discovered black hole, but they had been hit head-on by a huge meteorite, before they had gotten any where near their destination.

There had been a few space disasters since the space colonies had been built, but none had had any affect on Hattie and Jared's life until the one that involved their son Justin.

Due to the magnitude of the collision between the meteorite and Justin's space ship, all on board and their vehicle had been completely demolished. In other words, there were no human remains.

A National mourning service had been held at the N.A.S.A.'s head quarters in Virginia.

Hattie, Jared, Sonya, Jason, Ciaira and Chy-Chy had all been in attendance at the funeral service. It was the first time that security clearance had been given to Ciaira and Chy- Chy to visit Earth.

Justin's death had been a blessing in disguise. It had brought the White family, minus Justin, back together again.

Hattie's sadness at the loss of her youngest child, was some what lessened by the joy of seeing her now, almost grown, grand child.

Chy-Chy adapted very quickly to Earth and to her grandparents' home. In fact, she made herself right at home.

Hattie was finally able to give her only grand daughter, Chy-Chy, a doll that Hattie had had since she was a little girl. Hattie had named her favorite childhood doll, Molly. Molly had been found in an old barn on one of Hattie and her mother's antiquing trips, that Hattie just had

to have. Her mother, Jennifer, had bought it for her. The doll, Molly was dressed in an early 1900's costume, a blue and white gingham checked long ruffled dress with a white lacey pinafore and matching pantaloons. Molly also had small black laced up granny boots and a blue parasol. The doll was one of Hattie's most priceless possession. Her doll had always represented the life and time period that Hattie had always wished she had lived in.

Chy-Chy had never had a doll before. There was no such thing found on her mother, Ciaira's planet, Crystalmel. Even though Chy-Chy was a bit too old for a doll, she fell in love with it immediately and fondly called Molly her little sister. She promised her grandmother that she would treasure it forever.

Ciaira thought that life on Earth was quite primitive, but she fell in love with Earth's Zoos and Aquariums. She had never seen such life forms before, as there was absolutely no other life form on her home planet, other than her people.

Jason, Ciaira and Chy-Chy visited Earth for a year. This gave the White family plenty of time to really cement and bond their relationships with Hattie , Jared and Sonya.

Chy-Chy was also enamored by the zoos and aquariums. She begged to go see them daily, but had to be satisfied with weekly visits.

The whole White family had practically been taken over by the government and the media. Everyone wanted to meet and interview Ciaira and Chy-Chy. Sonya took on the role of interpreter for Ciaira and attended many government briefings with her.

The White family was escorted everywhere they went as they were considered the hottest story to hit the U.S. ever. They were treated as top priority for the complete year that Jason and his family were on Earth.

The only peace they found was in the comfort of Hattie's and Jared's home. At Hattie's home, Chy-Chy kept her grandparents entertained with all her wondrous talents and skills. Hattie and Jared were in constant awe whenever Chy-Chy moved things magically with her mind. She practically rearranged the whole condo by moving furniture and knick-knacks all around with just her mind. Chy-Chy would often sneak up behind her grandmother and levitate her up to the ceiling. Hattie would scream with surprise and then delight as the rest of her family would laugh and enjoy these escapades.

Hattie's home had not heard such laughter since her children were little. It was a joyful reunion for everyone.

The year passed quickly and soon Jason, Ciaira and Chy-Chy had to return to their space colony. As busy as their visit on Earth was, it was the best vacation they had ever actually had.

Chy-Chy wanted to stay with her grandparents and Hattie and Jared wanted her to stay also. But she couldn't. There were on-going tests that she was still required to finish at the space colony.

Jason told his daughter that once the novelty had wore itself out, she would be free of further obligations and then be able to visit her grandparents whenever she wished. Space travel was definitely not a problem for Ciaira or Chy-Chy due to their physical make-up.

Jason had assured his parents that there were only a few more years required until his and Ciaira's commitments with N.A.S.A. were completed. He had also told Hattie that there were about a dozen new bi-terracial children now living on the space colony, so much of the intense pressure was already off Chy-Chy. But her being the first and the oldest bi-terracial child, she was expected to check in periodically for monitoring of her life and progress at all stages.

Hattie had never thought in her wildest dreams that she would have been the matriarch of the most important Being in modern Earth's history. But that's what Chy-Chy was.

Fortunately for Chy-Chy, she loved the attention and realized her importance. She cooperated fully with whoever and whatever was needed. Even though she was now in the early years of adolescence, it never dawned on her to rebel.

Chy-Chy had inherited more of her mother's beings traits than of her dad's human traits. Crystalites didn't have any of the human foibles of insecurity, self-doubt, ego problems, low self esteem or identity crisis. They were brought up knowing their destiny and worth. Each Crystalite knew of their individual importance and were directed early on in to their life's work. They functioned for the common good of their fellow beings and society and were happy to do so.

As more and more bi-terracial children were integrated with Human beings, the better life would become. It would take some time before total integration was accomplished, but it would happen. As more and more Humans and 'Terri's' shared their lives, their combined knowledge would only enhance each other. Life would rise to higher and higher levels. Heaven would become closer than it is now through death.

Hattie now wished that she could stay alive long enough to witness all the fantastical major changes that would most certainly happen in the not to distant future.

Hattie had finally conquered her fear of changes.

Unfortunately, her Human life would soon be over.

48

Heaven

Angela had just recently reunited Hattie's son Justin with his grandparents, Jennifer and Bob. Angela still could not get over the beauty of witnessing these heavenly reunions. It seemed like it was only yesterday, so to speak, that she had goofed up Hattie's and Kaitlynn's lives. Yet everything in both of their lives had actually worked out quite well. God and His council members told her that 'it was as it should be', and they were right. And now for Angela to actually meet an off-spring of one of her two favorite baby-souls, well, it made her feel kind of like a Nana.

Angela rather liked the fact that she could still feel such motherly instincts, as she had never had the chance to be a 'physical' mother, but here she could still experience the mother- thing in Heaven. She figured that many spirits will learn in Heaven the things they hadn't had a chance to learn on Earth and vice versa. Knowing this calmed her soul and she hoped that this piece of knowledge would calm many restless souls on Earth. An Earthling may often not get to have some of the 'things' like motherhood on Earth, but any worthwhile experience that God wants most spirits to have will be given to them eventually. Many times, however, a Human is experiencing something that they want to experience in a very different, not as obvious way. For instance, if one does desperately want to be a parent but can't seem to physically carry a child, very often that person will find themselves in another situation where they are taking care of and nurturing a needy soul. This may be done in the actions of being some kind of teacher, nurse, role model, volunteer, a big sister or brother or even nurturing a needy spouse or family member. What one wants, one usually gets, but unfortunately, it is not always recognized at the time, that their 'prayer and want' were actually answered. It is often at a much later date when one is reminiscing or thinking in hind-sight, that one finally sees that they did indeed get exactly what they had previously asked for. God's ways are more often than not, very puzzling, but just as miraculous when one finally realizes that He did hear their prayer and answered them. No one is forgotten, no prayer goes unheard.

Angela had decided that until all of Justin's family and Kaitlynn's family were all together again in Heaven, she would keep a low profile. There was no need for her to spill the beans just yet.

In the mean time, Angela and the rest of the spiritual world, were in a fairly frenetic phase. There seemed to be a lot more activity in all the various spiritual planes. Especially in the 'ghostly' realm. There seems to be more ghost-sightings on Earth than ever before. Many spirits or 'ghosts' who left Earth in what appeared to be untimely situations, like through being murdered or through suicide, seemed to be stuck some where between Earth and Heaven.

What earthlings don't realize is that even after death, a spirit has free will and can choose to not come into Heaven. This choice is usually made because a spirit hasn't forgiven someone on Earth or themselves of some 'wrong doing'. Before they enter heaven they need to get through the anger and revenge negativity that they are still stuck in. Some 'ghosts' are full of shame at all the pain and hurt that they may have caused others, and until they can accept and forgive themselves they are apt to linger for quite some time in the level between Earth and Heaven.

This is where prayers can be helpful also. One should not assume that once a fellow Human being has died, especially in a very troubling way, that spirit may still need to be prayed for. This is why love and the act of forgiveness is so important on Earth (and every where else). It is not for us to make judgment , that is God's call to make. Many spirits are held in the middle or in a state of limbo because they have not been 'released' or 'let go' by those still on Earth.

When it is time for a Human to die and pass over, they must be let go. If a sad and grief ridden Human can't or won't let go, they are only hurting themselves and their loved one.

"Love them and leave them. If you truly love someone, let them go when it is time to let go," Angela prayed to all her fellow spirits. "You will all meet again." She wished that Human's would see how many chances they have to practice this act while they are still alive. Especially when a child reaches adulthood, be it to go to college or get married. When it is time for them to leave the 'nest', let them go with peace and love. The more adept a person gets at doing that the better prepared that person will be when it is time for themselves or a loved one to go to the next level. One can only go upward. It can be a very easy transition or a very difficult one, but that determination is in each person's individual control.

With the increase of communication and contact between Humans and Spirits, levels and planes tended to over lap. Much like when there's a change from low tide to high tide in the Earth's oceans. In comparison, it felt and appeared like a tidal wave spilling over the crumbling sea wall, or spilling over a spiritual level. Prior to the 21st century, hardly a ripple was ever seen or felt by the angels.

Angela supposed that this was good thing and part of god's Plan, "that there would be more and more unity between spirits and Humans." However, this was occurring in a much different fashion than Angela ever anticipated. She, like many Humans, always thought that there would be more of an apocalyptic type of reunion; an end of the world apocalypse thing. But Angela didn't think that way any more. The reunion seemed to be a much gentler event. She did like this concept much better.

The angels had been told by a council member, that the Complete Reunion of All Spirits was coming sooner than later. (But that could still be hundreds, maybe thousands of years, Earth-time, in the future.) No one but God really knew for sure.

But because things were becoming more chaotic in Heaven (although it was a good chaos), all the angels were 'on their toes', so to speak.

Another reason that Angela and her peers were so busy right now, was that the Humans were using more of their brains and thus, becoming more and more intelligent. Humans had recently learned that once an idea, or invention or new concept was either, literally, voiced and talked about out loud, or simply just thought about to oneself, that thought, idea, invention or concept, was released out into the Earth's atmosphere. Much like a radio transmitter sending out radio waves that were picked up either by satellites or a radio receiver, and then sent down to be received and heard by, whoever was tuned in to that particular radio station.

In other words, if two people are on the same thought wave-length, even if they are on opposite sides of the planet, they can technically pick up each other's ideas. Humans had been developing their individual mental telepathy skills on a one on one basis, for quite some time now. But, they were now finding out that these brain waves could travel at will, un-checked, to anyone open to or on the same brain-wave. Usually the receiver and transmitter were people at the same level of intelligence or at the same level of spiritual awareness.

The Human scientists were having a ball with this newly discovered Human capability, and were busy trying to process and document all the information, ideas and concepts that they had learned to intercept. (Picture the problem that humans had with the eavesdropping situation created by the over use of cellular phones, the numerous 'phone-waves' often over lapped and were received by any open cell-line near the same frequency.)

Earth's history has proven time and time again, that sometimes the least likely person could develop or invent the most important machine, drug, art, book, of its era, that would effect all of mankind positively. Many people have the same or similar idea that they discuss with a friend or colleague, yet don't know how to actually make it work or how to fund the idea. And then, maybe a year or so from then, they see their 'invention' or 'idea' on the market, and know that it was 'their idea'.

Angela and the angels often heard many of the 'jokes' from Earth. It seems like one person tells a joke and before you know it, everyone is repeating it all over the world. Jokes seem to spread as fast as an unchecked forest fire. Most of the 'clean' jokes were appreciated even in Heaven, as a sense of humor was a common trait of all Beings. God loved a good joke and loved to laugh. One only had to look at one's own life and surroundings to see some of God's humor.

Another reason that the spiritual levels were over-lapping, was because now, the majority of Humans were more spiritually aware than ever before. The non-believers were now in the minority. As a result of this change, the original negative bigoted climate on Earth had changed drastically. Things like abortion and protests against abortions was now a thing of the past.

An Aware Advanced Spirit also knows not to waste their valuable time on issues like the right or wrong of abortion. A spirit never dies, and cannot be 'killed' or 'murdered' by another. If a fetus is aborted or dies of natural causes in the womb, it is because the baby's spirit has chosen to not be born. The misinformed fanatics who 'judge' this incident as a horrible crime are merely ignorant of just what a soul is. Many baby souls are recalled to Heaven for reasons only known by God. Many young Humans die at what Humans feel are inappropriate or inopportune times, but there is always a reason and always a lesson to be learned. Many times it's a needed lesson to learn for someone. Whether Humans like it or not or can understand or not is not the issue. Question God as you will, but have Faith that there is a damn good reason why 'bad things happen to good people.' One just has to stop and take the time to figure it out and then learn from it. Like it or not, that's the way love (and life) goes.

A soul is an ever lasting being, regardless of what happens to the physical body. Period.

The more advanced a spirit is, Human or otherwise, the less racist, bigoted, homophobic, judgmental, mean, rotten, selfish, sinful, etc., etc., one becomes. The more advanced spirit is more loving, patient, understanding, compassionate, accepting, forgiving, etc., etc., and a much better being. The advanced Human spirit, being, becomes a truly good person naturally. Hence a 'good angel'.

And everyone knows that the better the social climate, the happier the people, (and vice versa.)

"Good begets goodness," said Angela. "That's a sure thing in Heaven as well as on Earth. It's something one can hang their hat (or halo) on!"

49

Kaitlynn

1971

Alantra was in the process of preparing her mother's house to be put up for sale. It was in a prime real estate area and there had already been plenty of offers. Alantra had been dragging her feet about selling it, as she had wanted to hang on to every part of her mother, Kaitlynn, that she could. Since her mother's death, Alantra had spent most of her spare time at the house. She was now over fifty years old, and although still a working nun, she found her self often visiting the house and loved to sit in her mother's favorite rocking chair reminiscing about the past.

Alantra was remembering Kaitlynn's 75th birthday party and the opportunity she had had to finally meet Jennifer. That meeting, which she had been responsible for arranging as a surprise for her mother, had done wonders for Kaitlynn's emotional well-being. Kaitlynn's depression ended that day and instead of a frown, a small lovely smiled graced her old lined face up until the moment she died.

Kaitlynn had passed away, quietly and gently two years ago on July 20, 1969.

It happened a couple of days after she, and the rest of the world, witnessed the historical event of Astronaut Neil Armstrong landing and walking on the surface of the moon.

After hearing Armstrong's famous statement, 'That's one small step for man, one giant leap for mankind ', Kaitlynn whooped with joy and laughter.

She had known since she was a young child, that some day somebody would fly to the moon,(and not just through a song). Everyone, especially Kaitlynn's parents, use to berate her for having such fanciful outrageous ideas. But Kaitlynn knew in her heart and soul (foreknowledge) that the idea of flying was not as farfetched as everyone else seemed to think.

Alantra had been with her mother, watching this historical event unfold on the television. She, too, had been a bit skeptical whenever she heard her mother talk about going to the moon.

Now that it had really happened, it made Alantra look at her mom with a bit of awe. She wondered how her mom could have possibly known that such an event would really occur. She started to think back over the years to see if her mother might have predicted any other earth shattering events.

Looking back, Alantra would see that her mother was kind of a visionary. Kaitlynn had worked hard and diligently for years for women's and children's rights. And now in the 1970's,the Feminist Movement seemed to be picking up where Kaitlynn's work had left off, and was bigger and more organized than ever before.

Alantra had also been at her mother's side when Robert Kennedy and Martin Luther King were assassinated. Alantra and her mom had spent many hours talking about civil rights and the negative racial climate that had taken over the American society. Kaitlynn often got antsy, wishing that she could travel to the South and join in the civil rights' cause. She believed that Black people should have the same rights, opportunities and equality as white people. This whole situation was reminiscent of the women's plight back in the early 1900's, that she had fought so hard, and successfully, helped to change.

Kaitlynn did manage to dictate a few articles, which Alantra typed up for her, encouraging all minorities, including women, to join together to form a larger, greater voice to help right these wrongs. Kaitlynn had no problem getting anything she wrote published, either through a newspaper or in a magazine. Her reputation and past writing successes guaranteed her an audience.

Alantra marveled at the number of dignitaries and famous people of the time, that had attended Kaitlynn's funeral. It had been one of the largest funerals that the city of San Francisco had ever witnessed. People came from all over the United States. Tanya and Jennifer flew in from New Hampshire, and stood with Alantra and her dad, Paul, in the sad receiving line. Many hours were spent at the reception which was held in Kaitlynn's beautiful big house, following the burial. Everyone talked and reminisced about Kaitlynn's wonderful life.

Tanya and Jennifer left knowing that they would probably never see Alantra or the West Coast again.

Alantra finally remembered and thought about Jennifer's parting words; "I'm going to name my first daughter Kaitlynn, after my Aunt Kate." Alantra knew how pleased and honored Kaitlynn would have felt about that. Alantra thanked Jennifer whole-heartedly for that promise, as she knew that Jennifer's child would be the closest her mother and father would ever come to having a grand child.

Alantra was also in the process of leaving her own mark on mankind, although it would be years before she really knew how important of a contribution she was making. Because of her mom's painful death from the ravages of scleroderma (although Kaitlynn died happy), Alantra had become interested in making the dying process as painless as possible for others.

She felt that people, young and old, who were suffering and dying from an agonizingly painful disease, should be made as physically comfortable and pain-free as possible, without being hooked up to life support machines. Her philosophy about pain-free-death would eventually become known as the Hospice Program.

Alantra took it upon herself to study and research death, both physically and spiritually. She wanted death to be approached intelligently and as free of negative emotions with the acceptance of its being just another cycle of life, by helping to minimize pain and the fear of dying for both the dying patient and the family and friends around the dying person.

She delved into the element of grief and the whole grieving process, that up until now, so many people couldn't seem to deal with. Alantra discovered that if the whole process of dealing with death could be approached by a team of doctors, nurses, personal care attendants, house keepers, social workers, clergy and family, where group therapy and support sessions were held regularly to discuss the managing of a dying person's final needs, the dying process became a group effort. The group effort and support that everyone shared in around the dying person seemed to ease much of the individual's distress, pain and grief a great deal. A group effort took the sole responsibility off the shoulders of either the patient or the family, and made the letting go almost a pleasant experience. It also seemed to get rid of the helplessness and guilt that is often felt by the dying patient and the family members. Ironically, the people involved together in a death-event seemed to feel that the experience was often very up-lifting as opposed to being just a sad painful affair.

Alantra tried to explain it by showing how so many people joined together at the time of the birth of a child, and with the same belief that death should be treated similarly, the whole life cycle would be better in the long run. If one stopped to think about the funerals they have attended in the past, many times the memories are quite pleasant as it was a chance to see many old friends and relatives that they hadn't seen for quite some time. But it's the mind-set that seems to be holding most people back.

It was a difficult concept for most to grasp, so Alantra concentrated in perfecting the Hospice program among her fellow nuns and the religious community. Because of their religion's belief about life after death, the nuns seemed more able to rid themselves of most of their own fears of dying.

The medical community had also been improving and discovering new and improved pain medications and procedures and were more than willing to assist Alantra with the pain management for end-stage or dying patients.

It would be a couple of decades before the Hospice concept would firmly take hold as an alternative way to die, but when it did, it would be one of the major milestones for humanity's spiritual growth.

Whether Alantra would know it or not, she was being guided and helped from Above.

Kaitlynn was still busy at work.

50

Hattie

2061

Hattie and Jared had moved into a senior center a few months ago. Hattie's husband had recently been diagnosed with Alzheimer's. The disease had come on very quickly and Jared now needed twenty-four care. The disease had taken them both by surprise as they had been use to and took for granted the good health they had both been blessed with for most of their eighty years.

Even though most of the Humans born after the turn of the century would live relatively disease-free, the last of the Humans born in the late 20th century still died from cancers, Alzheimer's, heart problems and other diseases that had been common in the late 1990's. Although the medical community had made wondrous strides in detecting and curing most diseases that had plagued mankind for many many years, there was relatively little that could be done for anyone born prior to the 21st century who had a predisposition of a genetic or hereditary disease. Now a days many diseases were cured in vitro through corrective genetic programming. Surgery could also be done to the fetus while still in the womb if any prior abnormality was detected before birth, if that was not possible and could not fix the problem, abortion would be the next accepted option. There were very few handicapped or retarded children born at this point in time.

Because married couples chose to stay together until 'death do us part', many healthy spouses lived with their sick partners. The healthy spouse usually opted for the clone service, so that they could still travel and visit friends and family, so the sick spouse was never left completely alone. The clones were a god-send, technically speaking.

Hattie had sought much medical advice and information regarding her husband's illness. She found out that there were now micro-chips available that could be implanted in the brain that could correct blindness and deafness. There was even a micro-chip available that could help control one's memory.

Hattie was trying to get the doctor's approval to install a memory micro-chip, with the hopes that the memories that Jared hadn't lost yet could be saved so that he wouldn't live out his last months in total dementia.

Part of Hattie was fearful of how she would or could exist without Jared by her side. She even considered seeing a lawyer to write up a Euthanasia pact before her husband got so bad that he couldn't sign his name.

She told her daughter, Sonya, about her fears and of her considering Euthanasia. Sonya begged her mom not to go that route, mostly because Hattie was still in good health.

Even at eighty, Hattie had no physical problems or limitations.

Sonya also suggested that Hattie could come and live with her, even though it was against the rules, because all seniors were suppose to reside in the senior centers. Sonya was now the Ambassador of the United States Extraterrestrial Embassy. She had become extremely important and a major authority on communicating with ET's, not only from Crystalmel, but many other planets and alien cultures as well. Because Sonya had perfected mental telecommunication between extraterrestrials and spirits of different planes, her talents and expertise were of the highest importance, not to mention, valued above all else that was happening in the world at this time. Sonya had actually become one of the most important people that had ever lived, especially of modern times.

As modest as Sonya was, she was just doing her job. There were many times in her life when she communed with Angela, lamenting about all the praise and glory that everyone was giving her. She didn't like or want all the responsibility that the whole universe seemed to be heaping on her shoulders. Angela was a great source of comfort and would periodically calm Sonya's concerns by telling her that God only gave people what they could handle, and that obviously God favored her and believed that Sonya could handle everything coming to and at her.

Sonya's communication skills would eventually become quite common place, as the world continued to evolve. There already was a group of extraterrestrial and Human scientists and engineers, who had learned through Sonya's training program, how to communicate together and were jointly working on developing a 'tru-cybor'. This was part being and machine.

A 'tru-cybor' would be able to travel and explore endlessly through space and would have the capabilities of communicating with any life form.

This invention was a direct result of the many people desirous of learning and honing in on Sonya's skills.

Hattie, knowing and being fully aware of her daughter's immense importance, knew that living with her daughter would hinder Sonya, and Hattie did not want to do that. She had never wanted to burden any of her children. Sonya, her husband, Kurt and their two sons, Colin and Tyler, had enough to contend with, without having an old lady live with them too. Most senior citizens felt that way which is why the senior centers came about. Hattie believed in loving them and letting them go and live their own lives. And her children certainly had done just that and in big and major ways. She was so very proud of them all. Her 'old fashion' ways had succeeded and surpassed all of her and Jared's expectations. She and Jared had lived a loving simple life. They had a wonderful family. All the modern technology and modern conveniences didn't change their good solid ethical values that they had lived by and taught their children.

Hattie compromised with Sonya by accepting tickets for a trip to Plymouth, Massachusetts. Sonya had made arrangements for Hattie and Jared to take a shuttle and then stay at one of the ocean front biospheres, which had the ambiance of an old fashioned sea side bed and breakfast inn, which had been very popular in the latter part of the 1900's.

Hattie had wanted to visit Kaitlynn's old home site for some time now. Ever since she and Kaitlynn had gotten to be great friends through Sonya's channeling skills, Hattie had been enthralled with Kaitlynn's history. Hattie had even taken it upon herself to research the history about the Plymouth, Massachusetts area in the late 1800's and early 1900's.

The day of the trip soon arrived. The shuttle picked Hattie and Jared, Jared's clone, and all their luggage up at the senior center. and proceeded to Plymouth, Massachusetts. The shuttle, being a hover-type helicopter craft, traveled smoothly and quickly from Plymouth, New Hampshire to Plymouth, Massachusetts. The trip took less than an hour.

After they arrived to the ocean biosphere, and after Hattie had gotten Jared settled and instructed the clone of its duties while she was gone, she prepared to take a walk into the town.

Plymouth, Massachusetts was a quiet sea side town and still a source of tourist attraction for many, as the Plymouth Rock, where the Pilgrims landed back in the 1600's, was still intact. Although Plymouth was completely encased in a bubble-dome, the ocean out side, though polluted, was still lovely to look at. Swimming was out of the question and recreational boats were a thing of the past. The erratic weather made sailing of any kind too dangerous. With modern air travel, sea travel had become obsolete. No one would even think to sit out in the sun and tan as the sun was far too hot and dangerous. The ozone layer had long ago disintegrated and as a result damaged most of the natural atmosphere.

But nevertheless, in the safety of the bubble-dome and biosphere, the ocean was a nice change for Hattie.

As Hattie walked to the out skirts of the town of Plymouth, she came across a small dilapidated farm house with a bronze plaque in front of it. It stated that 'This is the birth place of Kaitlynn Smith, a leader of women 1891-1969 A woman ahead of her time. She fought the good fight.'

Hattie sat down on a small cement bench in front of the plaque and marveled at where she finally was. She felt a sense of peacefulness and a feeling that she had finally come home after years and years of being away. It was an odd sensation, stronger than dejavu and a difficult feeling to comprehend.

Hattie thought about how much she had wanted to live back in the late 1800's and early 1900's. She thought that she would have liked to have lived in this very home. As old and run down as the small farm house was, it still looked inviting to her.

Hattie got up from the bench and walked to the front door. Surprisingly the door was not locked, so Hattie stepped in. The first thing she saw was a small gray kitchen full of its original, or what appeared to be original, fixtures; a wood burning stove, gas light fixtures and old rickety wooden table and chairs. They were definitely antiques and museum pieces of furniture and crude kitchen appliances that filled the small four rooms of Kaitlynn's old house.

Hattie dreamily walked through the small house, touching everything and trying to picture Kaitlynn and her mom and dad living in these tiny rooms. When she walked into the small bedroom and saw the old four poster feather bed she wondered if Kaitlynn had been born on that very spot. For a split second Hattie felt a pang of jealousy and melancholia. She wished that this had been where she had started her life.

After spending about an hour there, Hattie closed the door to Kaitlynn's home and slowly walked back to the inn.

She felt a sense of coming full circle, of completeness, that she tried to make sense of. Part of her felt that she had been cheated out of the life of her choice- a life similar to what her spiritual friend, Kaitlynn had lived. But the other part of her was grateful for all the wondrous adventures that she and her family had had in her life. She realized that she probably would have been happier if she had lived in the past, but that the life she did have now was pretty damn good. And God knows it had been a million times more exciting than what she had ever imagined as a child.

Hattie wished that she could talk about all this with her husband and best friend, Jared. But, Jared could not converse much any more.

Hattie decided that she could share this experience with her daughter Sonya, when she and Jared got back to New Hampshire. She also decided that she would get Sonya to channel Kaitlynn again so that she could tell Kaitlynn about her visit to her birth place. Hattie bet that Kaitlynn didn't know about the historical marker and plaque that had been put up on her home site in her honor and recognition of everything that she had contributed to America's women.

Hattie knew that this would bring a chuckle out of Kaitlynn.

After a few more days at the sea side inn, Hattie, Jared and the clone packed up to leave. On the shuttle trip back to Plymouth, New Hampshire, a horrendous thunderstorm struck and a lightning strike caused the shuttle to crash. There were no survivors.

Hattie died on July 20, 2061, exactly 92 years after Kaitlynn's death.

Needless to say, Sonya, Kurt, Colin, Tyler, Jason, Ciaira and Chy-Chy were devastated. But the funeral gave the White family another chance to reunite. The funeral was one of the biggest ever to take place on Earth. It was attended by all the Heads of States from both the planet Earth and the planet Crystalmel.

Ciaira's parents and most of the leaders from her home attended the funeral out of respect.

Hattie and Jared had never met Ciaira's parents while alive, but through their deaths, the two families became more united.

Sonya presided over the funeral, and with her communication skills, she brought the people of Earth and the beings of Crystalmel together in a stronger union that would remain solid throughout all of time.

Epilogue

Heaven

Angela's day of reckoning finally arrived. She was about to reunite her two favorite souls, Kaitlynn and Hattie. It was a cause for celebration. Angela went to great lengths to prepare a proper setting for the reunion to take place in.

She had summoned John and Mary and Jennifer and Bob ahead of time. Everyone was full of happy anticipation. Angela had found some extra tasks to keep Kaitlynn busy, as she had arrived in Heaven earlier, so that because of the power of a spirit's mental capacity to 'read minds', Kaitlynn wouldn't find out what was in store for her until Angela deemed the moment to be completely right.

Angela greeted Hattie immediately upon her arrival to heaven, while Jared was met by another angel and taken to meet his own waiting family.

Hattie recognized Angela simply by the exuberance and spectacular aura that surrounded her. Hattie also recalled her daughter, Sonya's description of Angela from all the

talks she had had with her. Her daughter's description fit Angela to a tee.

"Welcome, welcome, welcome!!" exclaimed Angela to Hattie with delight. "Welcome home!"

Hattie smiled gloriously as she flew to embrace Angela. She remembered Angela, also, from before she had gone to live on Earth. Hattie felt as though she was meeting an old best friend. Which is exactly what she was doing.

"It feels so wonderful to be back!" said an exulted Hattie. She then paused and sadly added, "Although I do miss my daughter, son and grand daughter."

"I know dear," said Angela with great compassion." But you'll all be together again soon enough."

Hattie brightened and nodded happily. "Oh yes, of course. How could I have forgotten that." As that heavenly knowledge swept through Hattie's newly arrived soul. A great sense of serene contentment cleared out all negative residue left over from her recently ended Earth experience. Hattie suddenly felt total love, warmth and a sense of belonging, like nothing she had ever felt on Earth. It felt glorious!!

"Hattie?" Angela said trying to get Hattie's full attention. For a moment Angela had forgotten the intense wondrous feeling a soul feels when it makes the transition from Physical to spiritual form. It is a major, major transformation and it takes a while for one to 're'-adapt to.

Although Angela knew of not one soul to ever have rejected this transformation. In fact, if a soul arrived too soon and was told that it had to go back to Earth, they often fought tooth and nail and returned back to Earth kicking and screaming, begging to be allowed to stay in Heaven. On the other hand, many times the angels would hear prayers from Earth, begging for more time on Earth. 'Please don't let me die,' was also a common request. But they never heard it from anyone who remembered being in Heaven.

Heaven was just that kind of place, where everyone wanted to be and wanted to stay.

Angela gave Hattie some more time to savor this magnificent moment.

After a bit, Hattie realized that Angela had been patiently trying to gain her attention.

"Are you ready for a real treat?" Angela said with a tone of great mirth and mischief.

Hattie first wondered how much better could this possibly get, but hearing the mischief in Angela's question, she became curious and wondered what else could be in store for her. "Sure I guess."

Angela then led Hattie into the most spectacular crystal chamber-room. Hattie was in awe at the magnificent beauty surrounding her. She then noticed another ethereal spirit before her. She immediately recognized and knew it to be her friend Kaitlynn. The two embraced as only spirits can, wholly and souly.

Kaitlynn and Hattie rejoiced at their long in coming reunion. Not only had they become friends on Earth through channeling, but they remembered that they had always been the best of friends. Their joyful reunion was soon cut short by the arrival of four more spirits.

Angela had to interrupt Kaitlynn and Hattie, by promising them that they would soon have tons of time to catch up later.

Kaitlynn and Hattie separated from their embrace, and turned to face the other spirits who had entered the crystal chamber.

"Mom! Dad!" said Hattie to Jennifer and Bob, as they all flew to embrace each other.

"Mom! Dad!" said Kaitlynn to John and Mary as they, too, flew into each others open embrace.

Then Hattie looked at John and Mary and exclaimed, "Mom! Dad!" Thrilled to see them also as they flew to embrace.

Kaitlynn also saw Jennifer and Bob and she too exclaimed with delight, "Mom! Dad!"

Suddenly Kaitlynn and Hattie, both a bit stunned, stopped and looked at both sets of parents. They then looked at each other questioningly, not fully understanding what had just happened.

"How can we both have the same parents, and two sets at that?" asked Kaitlynn and Hattie simultaneously with puzzlement on their bewildered angelic faces.

Even Bob, John, Mary and Jennifer looked some what confused.

Angela calmed every one down and once she felt some peace come back into the crystal chamber, she proceeded to explain about the mix up that she had made a long time ago. As Angela went on with her detailed explanation and her profuse apologies about her mess up, Hattie and Kaitlynn started to giggle and then burst out laughing whole heartedly.

Soon the parents joined in with the laughter as they figured it all out.

Angela's explanation had now made every weird, strange thing that had happened to all of them on Earth, very clear.

"No wonder I always wanted to fly," said Kaitlynn. "That's why my parents never really understood me."

"No wonder I always liked antiques and old things," exclaimed Hattie.

Now that Angela's 'secret' was out, Hattie, Kaitlynn, Jennifer, Bob, Mary and John could reenact their life experiences they almost had. They shared, through mental telepathy, each of their recent lives led on Earth with each other.

Jennifer, Kaitlynn and Hattie's sharing was particularly poignant, as Kaitlynn and Jennifer had actually physically met before Hattie had been born. Jennifer told Hattie how she had promised to name her first daughter Kaitlynn after her 'Aunt Kate'. The three of them understood the intricacies of there three lives easily because of their now heavenly nature.

(Had this been made known to them while all were on Earth, they all might have very well ended up in asylums, mostly because it was a bit confusing.) As the three of them realized how very connected they all were, their heavenly bond became that much stronger.

After all the now spirits had absorbed each others experiences, they realized that they had truly been enriched by the lives that they had actually lived on Earth. The fact that 'things' might have been different had Angela not messed up, really didn't amount to anything that earth shattering.

Kaitlynn and Hattie would still be best friends, but could now also consider themselves sisters. And both sets of parents are now also friends and can be considered as brothers and sisters or aunts and uncles as well as moms and dads.

Everybody is everything to each other. We are all our brother's keepers.

As Angela's reunion guests continued their sharing, Angela began to think about how many of Earth's different religious philosophies were often the fuel of wars and conflicts. She often wished that she could just pop down there at any time and explain how foolish they were being in this regard. She knew how some religions were fighting with the public school systems over the teaching of evolution as opposed to some religious beliefs of creationism.

When it came right down to it, evolution and creationism are exactly the same thing. Everyone, of all races, is related to everyone else, regardless if one took the stand point that Adam and Eve, or apes began humanity as is known today.

If someone is ignorant enough to dislike, or worse, hate a homosexual, or a person of a different skin color, then that person is truly hating his own mother, father, sister, brother, son or daughter.

Angela knew and was aware of how small brained many Humans were, and with small brains comes small and narrow thinking. But when a Human allows his brain to grow and be open and expand to more information, more acceptance, more love, the brain grows and can better assimilate and understand that we are all of the same roots and of the same being. Why it seems to be Human nature to shun anyone different from themselves, either physically or mentally, was so sad to Angela.

"We are ALL intricately connected!" Angela shouted into the universe.

Angela knew that there were large groups of people on Earth, who don't like it and don't want to be connected to everyone else, who appears different from them. But she knew that some where down the line they will have to grow up and deal with this reality. These dislikes all generate from the four letter word-FEAR "False Evidence Against Reality". Fear of the unknown.

"Well," thought Angela, "Find out about what you do not know. Study. Learn. Get with the program. Quit making life so much harder then it was ever meant to be. As they say, 'the only thing one needs to fear, is fear itself.' What do you think that means? Think about it. Figure it out. What have you got to lose? What are you all afraid of?"

As Angela watched Kaitlynn, Hattie and their parents wander off into one of the gorgeous beautiful Heavenly gardens to continue their sharing, Angela found herself contemplating all the 'firsts' that both Kaitlynn and Hattie had experienced in their lives. She realized that every single life one experienced on Earth and on other planets, would experience or be the first of something. One may be the first born, the first to go to college, the first to wed, the first to finish an exam in school, the first to solve a puzzle, the first to find a cure for AIDS, etc., etc.

Being first at anything opens the door to everyone around you. Sometimes a first can be good, but sometimes a wrong door is opened. But regardless, everyone serves a purpose, no matter how small or large that purpose may appear to a human, a purpose is a purpose and of great value to God. Yes it would be easier if Humans were all presented with an instruction book from A to Z, at birth that totally wrote out each person's game plan in plain and understandable language. It sure would save on a lot of pain and heart ache. But many many important life lessons can only be learned by either personal pain or the pain of someone around you. And these lessons are only painful because Humans make them painful.

Keep in mind that Heaven is also another level of learning trials. But the reason that Heaven is always referred to as a 'better place' is because once a soul arrives in Heaven, all the physical angst that humans suffer, disappears. There will no longer be all the physical distractions that hold so many captive down on Earth over and over again. In Heaven, one is relieved from all the excess baggage of a physical tangible world.

Heaven allows one to concentrate on one's knowledge, love and , spiritual growth. This is all done unencumbered by the physical need of food, drink, drugs, sex, aches, pains, gas, bowel movements, greed, disease, insects, unpredictable weather, lust, money, bills, taxes, cheats, liars, abusers, murderers, preachers, enemies, days, hours, minutes, weeks, months, years, aging, etc., etc.

The closest thing to Heaven that a Human can experience is when two people unite together, sharing complete true unconditional love. This can be found in a loving trusting physical relationship between two lovers, or found when people share deep intimate conversations and feelings in true two-way communication. These glimpses of Heaven are, unfortunately on Earth, often fleeting, but that wonderful feeling one gets when they did truly connect is remembered and sought after one's whole life. That search often leads a person off on the wrong tract of promiscuous sex, to false cult leaders, or into a drug addiction by self- medicating the pain away.

When one cannot find that 'piece of Heaven' on Earth, one often becomes angry and frustrated at the world in general, but the world being too big to attack, one then funnels these negative emotions towards violence, crime, hatred and blaming on others. Some will only 'attack' themselves with misery and self-loathing.

The answers are so simple, yet it seems to be human nature to not accept or look for simplicity.

Heaven could be on Earth if humans would take the time to find it, nurture it and spread it.

Angela desperately wished that she could give each and every human the answers to all their questions, and prove to them beyond a shadow of a doubt that God and Heaven are real, but she knew and accepted that it was only God's call to make as to where and when each human figured it all out. God's gift of free will to all beings was a curse in some ways as well as a blessing in disguise. But it was too apparent to Angela that most humans just didn't or couldn't seem to understand what a glorious gift free-will truly was.

The best that Angela could do is to explain that life and time on Earth is similar to a tornado. (Another analogy is the movie THE WIZARD OF OZ. God often inspires earthlings with certain life answers to many questions. One only needed to look with an open mind. The answers are there!)

Everything is spinning in circular cycles. Picture Heaven being the top or widest part of a tornado, and then each level or cycle or spin of the tornado is a particular time line. The smallest point can be called the beginning of time and the middle could be called the 1800's and the closest one gets too the Heaven area is modern time.

In other words, every time period is staggered, yet happening at almost the same time just on a different level. We are all, and have always been, in the tornado together. (Which can be a good or bad thing, because the trick is to get out of the storm.) "What goes around comes around" is a good truism. Perhaps once we all stop our lives from spinning out of control, the tornado will no longer make one dizzy and confused, and all the turmoil and upheaval on Earth will stop. But everyone, being connected, has to stop the spinning of their own personal lives FIRST.

Angela also wanted to share her thought, that although many Humans wished that they were in another place at another time, A SWITCH IN TIME won't always solve the problem that a Human must go through to find their own inner peace.

"Good luck! I'll see you soon," says Angela with God's love in her heart, as she went to join the others in the garden.

About the Author

Born May 27, 1952, a New Hampshire native with roots going back to 1644. Have one daughter, Sonya. In the process of building own home with partner, Dan, in Washington, NH. Previously published novel— *The Kiss Of Judas* in 1996.

Printed in the United States
90051LV00004B/183/A